'A vivid, richly inhabited account which rings with authenticity'

CYNAN JONES, AUTHOR OF *COVE*

'Taut, poised and powerful. Hunt has produced something truly special: a novel that both broods and races, and which tells us vital, troubling and hopeful things about ourselves'

CHARLES FOSTER, AUTHOR OF *CRY OF THE WILD*

'A rich and accomplished reimagining of Aztec colonial history'

EM STRANG, AUTHOR OF *QUINN*

'Nick Hunt deftly pulls off a delicately embroidered tale of what so easily might have been. A feast of language and imagination, brimming with very real detail and insight'

BENEDICT ALLEN, AUTHOR OF *EXPLORER*

'A novel of great originality, humanity and quest'

DAN RICHARDS, AUTHOR OF *OUTPOST*

'Immersive, transporting and spectacular'

FIONA MOZLEY, AUTHOR OF *ELMET*

RED

SMOKING

MIRROR

NICK HUNT

Swift

SWIFT PRESS

This paperback edition published by Swift Press 2024
First published in Great Britain by Swift Press 2023

1 3 5 7 9 10 8 6 4 2

Maps by Sue Gent, www.suegent.com

Text design and typesetting by Tetragon, London
Printed and bound in Great Britain by CPI Group (UK) Ltd, Croydon, CR0 4YY

A CIP catalogue record for this book is available from the British Library

ISBN: 9781800753235
eISBN: 9781800753228

In fourteen hundred ninety-two
Columbus sailed the ocean blue
He had three ships and left from Spain
He sailed through sunshine, wind and rain

ANONYMOUS

We eat of the earth
Then the earth eats us

NAHUA SAYING

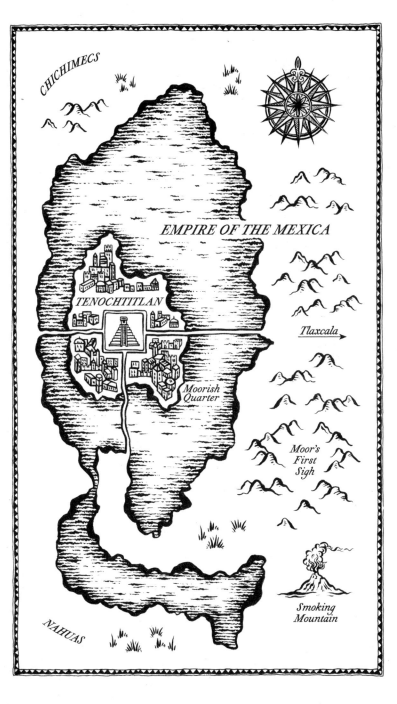

897

1492

13 KNIFE

*W*e were seven weeks at sea, but I do not like to think of it. In truth I do not remember much but flooded decks and storms at night and a ragged steady howl and the suspicions of the crew and waking up in fear. I sailed in the foremost ship. The other ships came behind. The greasy waves rolled against the hull and broke in cannon-blasts of foam and everything was always slick and I always had the sickness.

At sunrise and at noon and in the afternoon and at sunset and at night the faithful faced towards the east, which was the direction of the home that all of us had left. Their prayers went whitely with the wake. I alone faced to the west, as I am facing still.

We were seven weeks at sea and then came distant flocks of birds, so small I took them for flies at first. Strange, that I would see flies before birds. Then my eyes found their range. There was a pale heap of land resolving itself from the sea, separating from the sky. I watched as it became itself, as nothing became something.

A sailor standing near to me was the first of us to shout, and then the other men were shouting out from ship to ship and some of them were singing. I blocked my ears to the noise. The solemn bunching of the clouds. I knew an uncovering was at hand and I wanted some quiet within me. But then the horses sensed the land and started thumping in their stalls, and from high up on the mast a man cried God is great! The quietness could not endure. So it was that the ships of the caliph crossed the Sea of Darkness.

The gunwale's weathered wood was cool and wet beneath my hands. My clothing, when it brushed my skin, was so hot it burned. As we met the island's swell my stomach wallowed with the sickness that had ailed me for days and I hung from the prow, a figurehead, and heaved into the foam. No one saw me retch and spit. They did not regard me. As the anchors rattled down I studied the pale depths below, where silver fish were taking morsels of what I had expelled. This was my first offering to the New Maghreb.

When I raised my eyes again I saw what the others saw, and like them I understood nothing of what it was. The green of trees. The white of sand. The black of rock. The white of surf. And against the surf the swarm of mushrik kanoas, sharp and dark, as they slipped from their coves to meet us.

927

1521

3 HOUSE

· ONE ·

S HE takes me by the hand and says, The smoke is on the mountain.

It is only cloud, I say.

It is more than cloud, she says.

We have come to the place of willow trees to watch the caravan depart. But the call has not yet come and so we watch the mountain. The mountain stands beyond the lake, its slopes rising bare and blue, the same parched colour as the sky. The lake is dull because the sun has not yet met the water.

We stand together looking up at the far naked peak. A foaming whiteness spews and rolls, clings to the mountain's sides. My wife has younger eyes than I.

It is smoke, she says again.

Perhaps, I say.

She is seldom wrong.

Do you hear it speak? she says.

We stand together listening. I do not hear the mountain. All I hear is the morning wind, the cry of a bird

I cannot name, the gentle lapping of small waves against the floating gardens.

No, I say.

It is sleeping now. But it spoke last night, she says.

My wife goes to the waterside and dips her ankles in. The water's skin appears to flinch as if it is repulsed. She tweaks the hem of her white dress and steps a little deeper in. Bright bubbles break the surface.

It spoke while you snored, she says, without looking back at me. The water laps her calves, her knees.

Not too far in, I say.

I am mistrustful of the lake as I was mistrustful of the sea. For a man who has drifted far I do not like the water. A mountain does not speak, I say, correcting her as I do with declining frequency these days. A mountain rumbles, booms or roars. It does not possess a voice.

Everything speaks, she says.

Thigh-deep now, her dress held high, she wades along the shallow shore. The floating beds are fulsome with crops before the harvest. Idly, as if thoughtlessly, she snaps off a cob of maiz and proffers me some yellow grains.

When I shake my head she shrugs and casts the maiz on the water.

A mushrik boy is watching us. Bare-footed, with a shaven skull, six or seven years of age, he is lurking in the trees where the road forks to the city gate. He might be hunting rats or water-gods.

I smile and call a greeting.

At first I think I am the cause of the fear on his face. I am used to this. Such fear is innocent. But his eyes are on my wife and the maiz floating on the lake. That wanton, wasted offering.

My wife's gaze fixes on him.

The child appears caught in fright but my wife speaks a word I do not know, something sharp that releases him, and he vanishes among the trees. The maiz bobs up and down. Ripples slowly spread from it, rolling out across the lake. I feel uneasy watching them, as I do increasingly.

Men are made of maiz, she says.

We are made of dust, I say.

Water glistens on her shins as she wades back onto shore. A slimy stripe of green weed is stuck between her toes. My eyes climb to the peak again, to the cloud-smoke bulging from its snout.

My man of dust, says my wife.

And with that I am joyful.

The rising sun has cleared the hills. Light spills across the valley. The dark lake turns to silver shards, scintillating blindingly, and the ripples from the broken maiz portend nothing more than peace rolling out across the world, its circles ever widening. The two of us are standing here at its very centre.

I am happier here, a foreigner, than I have been anywhere.

We stand together in the light. Her hand joins my hand.

Then from behind us comes the call, a single ululating voice, followed by the clash of drums and the twang of stringed instruments, and then the cries, the groans of beasts, the clattering hooves, the dust, the din.

We turn towards the city gate. The caravan is leaving.

*   *   *

The mushriks say it is the greatest sight in all of Mexica. Six hundred camels swaying through the gate of Tenochtitlan. Out they come in single file, their loads stacked high upon their backs, their lips curled back, their eyelids low, with expressions of great suffering. Red pom-poms bounce around their necks. Green banners fly above them. Twelve cavalrymen ride ahead on shining black and chestnut mares, then a herald with a horn, and behind him strides the first camel, and the second, and the third. One camel-driver hacks and spits. Another plucks an oud. The causeway shudders with the beat as they mount the floating road that connects the city to the shore, where the smoking mountain lies. And beyond the mountain, the high pass that is called the Moor's First Sigh. And beyond the pass, the brown plains, the verdant coast, the shining sea.

And beyond that, Andalus.

The caravan is bunched up now, the camels loping nose to tail, but once it has crossed the floating road it will elongate for miles. The dust of its passing can be seen from fifty miles away, they say.

The ugly deer! the mushriks cry.

They call our horses swift deer and our camels ugly deer.

Atop the humps of the ugly deer are balanced tough, sun-hardened men, undulating with their loads, brandishing long whips. Camel-drivers from the sandy deserts of the Old Maghreb, I should think of them as my countrymen, but they are another breed.

Peace be with you, I call, seeing one I recognise. He mutters something back.

At times these men are hostile because of what I am. A dhimmi, a protected person and a person of the book, but not a person of the faith. I am like them but not like them. I do not judge their prejudice. If there is one thing I have learned it is how not to judge.

My wife stands next to me, watching in the way she does. Her expression seems far away but I know she is noting everything. The camel-drivers look at her and then quickly look away.

A charm against the evil eye hangs around one camel's neck. Around another, a star and moon.

A hooded baggage guard slides past with an arquebus across his knees.

The procession rumbles on and on. The mushriks laugh and stare.

In those swaying camel-bags are bales of the finest cloth, ayate fibre, dried tubaq, quetzal feathers, jaguar skins, ornately worked jade ornaments, obsidian, silver, powdered gold, tortoiseshell, tomatl seeds, balls of uli, amaranth and Mexica's other wondrous goods.

Yours are coming, says my wife.

She counts the loads as they go past, forty packs on forty beasts, marked with the sigil of my house.

The greatest shipment we have sent. My fortune in xocolatl.

My wife says something in her tongue, a prayer to the Lord of the Nose, god of merchants and travellers, whose symbol is a bunch of reeds.

God protect you, I say to my xocolatl.

Behind the camels come scores of mules roped one behind the next, backs bent beneath their loads. Strong deer, the mushriks call them. And at last some Berbers herding sheep, which are not bound for the sea but for the fertile pastureland between this valley and the coast, where they will graze under guard. They will return as meat and wool for the markets of the city.

The caravan is on the lake. Its head has reached the furthest shore.

Dust hangs in the air behind, collapsing like a blanket.

For twenty years I have watched these caravans leave and return, and it is still a miracle.

It is my miracle.

We turn our backs on the lake and look towards the city gate. It is the Gate of the South, of the Left-Handed Hummingbird. His sullen idol squats above, grimacing like a child. A flaming sun stands over it.

Together we walk beneath.

My wife's name is Malinala, which means Woman of the Grass. She was born a Nahua slave but has been much elevated.

My name is Eli Ben Abram. I have been elevated too. I was born a dhimmi, a Jew in the Caliphate of Andalus.

We make an unusual coupling as we pass along the streets, through the sunlight and the shade, on bridges over green canals. She in her white dress and me in black with my bleached skullcap, sun-damaged, sweating through my beard. She is young and I am old, between us almost thirty years.

But this is a city, and an age, of unusual couplings.

The air feels disturbed from the passing of the caravan. Everyday city life is filling back in behind. A woman with black shining braids is sprinkling water on the dust, tamping it down with her feet. A man sits in the shade with a heap of spoiled kasava. We pass the Street of the Artisans and the Place of the Obsidian-Polishers, past the vegetable marketplace and the shrine to the Dog-Headed God, darkly stained, alive with flies. A naked child plays near it. Down a long stone avenue I catch a glimpse of some great lord passing in his palanquin, carried by costumed slaves, like a distant feathered bird.

From far away comes music and a smudge of purple smoke.

We come to the Moorish Quarter marked by the Caliph's Gate, which is an archway made of mud. The archway is a symbol as is so much else. The usual man is standing guard, chewing on some kind of root which makes him salivate green juice. The cobblestones around his boots are splattered with expectorations.

He greets me punctiliously, lowering his scimitar. There is a scrape upon his cheek as if he has been fighting.

All is well? I ask.

Well enough, he answers.

The courtyard, deserted at this time, has not yet flooded with scalding light. The sun will take another hour to clear the steep stone buildings. Butterflies meander over stunted citrus trees in pots. The broken fountain gurgles, its workings gummed with slime. Shoes are lined up by the mosque, beyond which is the synagogue, protected by the caliph's law.

The caliph's law reaches even here, across the Sea of Darkness.

I unlock the door to our rooms with the key I wear around my neck. The lock and key I ordered all the way from Qurtubah. The mushriks do not have locks like ours, as they do not have keys like ours. Their locks and keys are invisible. It takes time to understand them.

First I must do the paperwork relating to the caravan. Columns in ledgers must be filled, stamps stamped and seals sealed. I work at my small desk in the corner of the largest room, where the daylight penetrates. Candles are in short supply and expensive here. While I write, Malinala heats the pan to toast the beans.

When the smell reaches me, great happiness arises.

This is the finest hour, while the faithful are at prayer and there is no one to demand that I attend to this or that. No requests, beseechments, emergencies or questions. Just me at my desk and Malinala at the pan, goading the embers into flame. The scrape of the pestle as it grinds. The bubbling of water.

Next to my accounts of trade, and vastly more significant, are the chronicles of my travels in the New Maghreb. Twenty-nine battered tomes, one for every year. Beside them are my lexicons in Arabic and Mayayan, Mayayan and Nahuatl, Nahuatl and Arabic, without which I would not be here. Without which we would not be here.

Malinala stirs the pan and pours in boiling water.

How long? I ask in Nahuatl.

Too long, she says in Arabic.

Just a silly game we have.

This is the finest hour.

Also gathered on my desk are the part-translated codices, the glyphs of flowers, feathers, flames, houses, serpents, spears and rain, the squat, squared pictograms I have copied where I find them. And my notes upon the calendar with its day-counts and its year-counts, its interlocking wheels of time, a system of intricate and immense complexity that I am a poor student of, having no one to teach me.

There are those, both Moor and Mexica, that would call this heresy.

On the high shelf on the wall are the other precious things I own. My Torah and my Qur'an, wrapped in their black velvet. A gold menorah made for me by the Mayayans of Yuqqatan as a parting present years ago. A conch-shell from the Qarib Sea. And an iron chest containing the papers that not even my wife has seen.

How long now? I ask.

Long enough, she says.

I put my pen and ink away and close the balance book. This year's caravan is gone. For the morning I can rest. By the window is a divan that receives my body now.

My wife brings the steaming cup. The steam is lanced by sunlight.

First I bring it to my nose and slowly, sumptuously inhale. It is like standing at the edge of a sweet, dark cloud.

I bring the cup to my lips and perform the first sip. It scalds. I take one burning gulp.

My heart expands. My blood thumps. Everything seems ringed with light. The dark cloud envelops me. I close my eyes.

The xocolatl does not bring sleep. It brings vigour and energy. It sharpens every sense, unblunts the dullness of the world. But my habit is to recline and let its life course through me.

I allow myself one cup a day. Others indulge more freely. For the Mexica of Tenochtitlan this drink is strictly circumscribed, drunk only at certain festivals or regularly by the priests, the noble lords, the emperor, who has the status of a god. The common folk might pass their lives without so much as smelling it.

They frown upon our appetites. But we are greedy people.

And now the xocolatl beans are packed and shipped across the sea, to be imbibed in lands the mushriks can barely conceive of. In Andalus and the Old Maghreb, the Christian kingdoms of the Franks, in Genoa, Venice, the Levant. And the dirhams flow back west to fill columns in my ledgers.

I think of the swaying camel-bags, in the foothills of the mountains now. Tomorrow they will cross the pass of the Moor's First Sigh.

I think of perfumed viziers in the great cities of Andalus, sipping xocolatl by fountains or in shaded orange groves. It is rumoured that the caliph himself takes it on occasion.

Malinala hums a wordless tune as she lifts the cup away. She lies down next to me, her head upon my arm.

It is a time of stillness now. After the ascent, the fall.

I forget about the broken maiz and the smoking mountain.

Dhimmi, comes the voice again.

It is the second or third time.

Wake up, dhimmi, the voice repeats. The council has been called.

Opening my eyes, I find that the sunlight has moved across the wall. It must be some time after noon. I feel stunned and bewildered. My arm is dead because my head has crushed the blood out of it.

Malinala is not in sight. My mouth tastes foul and bitter.

In the open doorway stands the silhouette of a man. I recognise him as a middling merchant of tubaq. He lingers there awkwardly, unsure of the etiquette, embarrassed to discover me asleep.

It is starting now, he says.

Though I am already dressed, I ask him for some time to dress. He departs thankfully after making a clumsy bow.

When I stand I find myself still half-caught in a land of dreams but I cannot hold onto them. I have never remembered dreams.

I splash water on my face and run a comb through my beard. I am unaccustomed to sleeping in the daytime.

Malinala? I call.

She is not in the smaller room, or the room in which we sleep.

She must have business somewhere else. It has always been this way.

Something vaguely troubles me, as small things seem to do these days. Perhaps it is my age and the small pains in my bones. Dhimmi. They did not used to call me that, not as a manner of address. They used to call me by my name, as I call them by theirs.

It is not a term of disrespect, but it is not not disrespect.

It does not mean anything. No matter what they call me.

By tradition the merchants' council does not meet in the Moorish Quarter but above a warehouse in the district of the jade-mongers. The jade-mongers are Zapotecs from a country far to the south, so they are strangers here like us, though we are much more strange. They speak a language of their own that I do not understand and Malinala does not understand, and keep themselves to themselves in guilds that permit no one in, not even the Mexica. The city is strictly zoned according to nation, rank and trade. In this sense it is similar to the cities of Andalus.

That is why we meet there, as foreigners among foreigners. It is by the emperor's dispensation, as is everything.

The walk to that district takes me through the city's narrow northern streets, away from the grand public centres of commerce and ceremony. The road is made of mud, not stone. The canals are brown and stagnant. An old woman with blue teeth is grilling fish from the lake beside a pool of effluence, causing me to step around. Oil spits from their charred skins and blind, pale eyes.

The distance is not so great but I wish I had a mule. But we are forbidden from riding deer within the city.

As a dhimmi, I was once forbidden from riding deer in Andalus. But when I came to the New Maghreb many things became possible. The first time I rode a horse was on the island of Qubah, as our delegation went to visit an important chief. I cannot now recall his name. There have been many names.

Two mushrik labourers barge past with bales of rushes on their backs, stooped double as they walk. They do not even see me.

From the dimness of his shop an artisan glances up, alarmed, a hammer and awl poised in his hands. Before him lies a stone mask, its face an unearthly green.

A gang of children follows me, three boys and two girls. The younger girl appears to wander in a kind of daze. Her mouth hangs like an idiot's. Dust is in her hair. I cannot keep from glancing back to watch her as she stumbles on. Her companions leave her behind. I leave them behind.

The warehouse is for storing grain, which covers the floor in mounded dunes. I am sweating as I climb the stairs. The door is unattended.

The room is spacious, unadorned, with squat pillars around its walls. Dusty sunlight falls like golden soup on those assembled. A few familiar faces nod to me, then turn away. The formalities must be done. The council is in session.

Thirty men are gathered here, some cross-legged, some on stools, some in simple skullcaps and some in turbans of bright cloth, some clean-shaven, some moustached, some with orange-hennaed beards. Small jewels gleam in earlobes. Teaspoons twirl in glasses. Some wear their fortunes on display, others keep their wealth concealed under plainer travelling clothes, but all these men have influence. In the middle of the floor stands Abd al-Wahid Ibn Nasr.

Come, Eli, he says, gesturing to an empty seat.

I glance at the man who called me dhimmi, but he is shuffling papers.

You have not missed much, says Abd al-Wahid. Reports on this morning's caravan. Market rates, the usual things. One of the kasava sellers has been cheating us again. But we have something bigger to discuss. We have word of Benmessaoud.

There is a stirring in the room but not much more than that. As if a breeze has whispered through and quietly departed.

Some xocolatl is going round, but from its smell, even from here, I can tell that it is badly made. The beans are burnt. Not enough chilli. Too much tlilxochitl-pod. I decline and accept instead a glass of tea from a silver pot with a spout shaped like an elephant's trunk. The tea falls in a slender stream, bringing mint and sweetness.

Our informants say he crossed the sea a month ago, says Abd al-Wahid. We do not know if he resupplied in Qubah or Yuqqatan. But now it appears that he has sailed much further up the western coast. The Mayayans counted sixteen ships.

He is coming, then, says someone.

He might be coming, says someone else. The New Maghreb is vast enough. Might he not be tempted somewhere else?

All roads lead to Mexica, says Abd al-Wahid.

Abd al-Wahid is dressed in a loose brown robe and a turban of bleached ayate cloth, plain but for a quetzal feather pinned at its centre. His heavy face runs into jowls. He wears a snowy beard. He is a substantial man, both tall and fat at the same time, his body cushioned generously. Of the thirty merchants in this room, he is one of only three who came here in the founding fleet.

The second of them, Mohammed Issa, wears a robe of brilliant green with Mexica patterns around its hem. He is sitting with his eyelids closed. Perhaps he is asleep.

The third of them is the dhimmi who has just poured tea.

All the rest have departed now, some years ago, some decades. Some returned to Andalus with fortunes either lost or made. Some remained in Qubah to act as middlemen. Others travelled west, or north, in search of cities made of gold, or to establish trading posts, and else returned or did not. Others died and were buried here, with their faces towards Makkah.

We must assume he is coming, says Abd al-Wahid. Or at least that he intends to come. The Tlaxcalans will surely direct him here, as they did with us. The question is what he will do when he gets here. And what the emperor will do.

When did you last see the emperor? asks one of the younger merchants.

The question is directed at me. I feel the weight of eyes.

I pause to take a sip of tea. Too much sugar. Not enough mint.

I think about Malinala.

Eli? says Abd al-Wahid. When did you last see Moctezuma?

It has been some months, I say. I believe the last time was before the Festival of Rain.

And was he in good health? he asks.

He was not in bad health, I say.

You used to visit more frequently, says a silver merchant from Gharnatah. Why has he not sent for you? Did he grow bored of your company? Did you displease him in some way?

Not as far as I know, I say.

And what did you talk about? he asks.

For the most part, backgammon.

At this there is general laughter.

It is not a joke, I say.

Thank you, Eli, says Abd al-Wahid. The emperor mentioned nothing of a Moorish army crossing the sea?

He did not, I say. But he has spies and messengers like us. Perhaps even the same spies and messengers.

Ha! cries the silver merchant, though no one else reacts.

Abd al-Wahid stalks the room with his big hands clasped behind his back. On his feet are slippers of gold brocade, pointed at the tips. There are rings upon his fingers and a pendant around his neck, a pale green stone that holds the light.

We have a careful balance here, he says, stepping here and there. Benmessaoud will tip the scales.

That goat-fucker, someone says.

There is uproar in the room.

Please, protests Abd al-Wahid, but everyone is talking at once.

Fanatics, illiterates! cries the merchant next to me. Why would the caliph send them here?

They are men of God!

Of gold, more like...

Bandits! Plunderers!

Mohammed Issa opens his eyes and stares around, bewildered.

Peace! bellows Abd al-Wahid. You are worse than drunken Christians!

By degrees the clamour subsides.

I take another sip of tea.

A water-pipe has now appeared, its bowl filled with tubaq leaves. Drinking smoke is not a habit I have ever taken to. The first time I attempted it, it made me cough until I cried. It made me almost as sick as I had been at sea.

But people are drinking smoke these days across the caliphate, they say, even on the steps of the Great Palace at Qurtubah.

The burnt xocolatl is passed one way, the bubbling water-pipe the next. Everyone is chewing sunflower seeds and spitting their husks upon the floor. I see the scene through the eyes of the Mexica.

Through the eyes of Benmessaoud.

We are greedy people.

A fly is circling the room, bumping against the pillars and walls. From outside, from far away, drifts the sound of flutes and drums.

Eli? says Abd al-Wahid.

The weight of eyes again.

Sorry, I did not hear, I say.

We would like you to go to the Black House to converse with the emperor. Try to gauge his state of mind. Find out what he knows, whether he knows anything.

Well, we can try, I say.

If Benmessaoud's army comes, will he open the gates of the city or will he keep them closed? Will he sink the floating roads?

We will see what we can learn, I say.

And Eli, he says quietly, you should leave your wife at home.

The assembly seems to stir again, touched by another passing breeze.

My wife is my mouth, I say.

At this there are a few coarse laughs from the vulgar-minded in the room.

My voice, I say. She is my voice.

Abd al-Wahid looks sad. You speak Nahuatl well enough, he says. You have your own voice now.

When I step outside, the drifting music of the flutes and drums has ceased.

A hairless dog stands watching me, its ears alert, grotesquely bald, its skin the colour of blue maiz. I give the creature a wide berth, as would a Moor of any faith, and hope it does not follow me. It does not follow me.

On my way back through the streets I see the little girl again. The one who seemed an idiot, wandering behind her friends. She is alone, crouched on the ground, examining a flat stone.

Her posture makes me curious, so I divert towards her.

When I am standing over her I see that she has prised the stone from a nest of black ants, revealing the corridors they have made in the soft brown earth. The ants teem in emergency patterns and the little girl watches them.

Her face and arms are marked with livid blotches, pink and puce.

Good sun, I say in Nahuatl. She does not look up.

She is holding what seem to be grains of white rice. As I watch she adds another to the growing pile. They are not grains of rice but the eggs of the ants, which she lifts between finger and thumb while using a small stick to fend the ants away.

What are you doing, child? I ask. Still she does not look at me. But her hand becomes a fist, hiding the eggs from my eyes as if they were a treasure.

Another man is standing guard with the usual man who is standing guard. I have not seen this man before. He is slight, narrow-faced, with a shaven upper lip.

All is well? I ask. I am not in the mood for talk but the question is a courtesy.

All is well, says the usual man. He steps aside to let me pass. The gnawed root protrudes from his teeth like a ravaged bone.

Peace be with you, says the other man.

And with you, I answer.

Where do they come from, these new men? I have given up keeping record. Every year they come and go, carried back and forth across the world, as if the caravans are rivers picking them up and placing them down. I used to greet them personally, inscribe their names in the chronicles. Merchants, traders, travellers. Now I hardly even notice them.

Your wife is back, he says.

Midway through the Caliph's Gate I am brought up short. My wife? I say.

The woman in white. The, uh...

My wife, I say.

Yes, he says. She passed this way about half an hour ago.

A yellow lizard is creeping across the wall behind his head. The afternoon is very hot. Light dazzles off the buildings.

Why are you telling me this? I ask.

I thought you would like to know, he says.

His manner is perfectly polite. I look into his eyes but detect no guile, no mockery.

The lizard halts, advances, halts.

Very well, I say, confused.

A moment passes and no one speaks. Someone is chopping wood somewhere, a sound that is both sharp and dull. I imagine that each of us might be marking the blows inside our heads, counting up or counting down.

The lizard resumes its crawl, heading towards the shadow.

Excuse me, says the narrow-faced man. I know it is not my concern. But we heard the drums today. Has there been a Flower War?

The usual man shifts his weight from one foot to the other foot. He sucks the root between his teeth.

What is that thing? I ask him.

They sell them in the marketplace, he says. It has a pleasant taste.

There is always a Flower War, I say to the other man.

The lizard has delved into a crack, leaving nothing but its tail.

The upright scimitar declines.

And you are right, I say. It is not your concern.

Malinala is in the smallest room, dressed, as the man observed, in white. You have been with the merchants, she says.

I do not know how she knows these things but she always knows these things.

I sit down upon my chair and take my sandals off. They are in the mushrik style, with soft-hard uli soles.

Yes. Now I am tired, I say.

Shall I wash your feet? she says.

I hesitate, then submit. Having my feet washed by my wife is one of my great indulgences.

She goes out into the yard and fetches a deep bronze bowl. Into the bowl she pours soap brought all the way from Andalus, from the luxurious bathhouses and steam-rooms of the caliphate. The room is filled with the smell of roses, flowers that she has never seen.

She mashes the water into foam and gently takes my ankle. Her fingers slip between my toes.

That is nice, I say.

So how were the Old Men of the Nose? she asks. The name is a joke we have, from the god of merchants and travellers.

The dust and grime of Tenochtitlan commingles with the water.

The same as they ever were, I say.

Were they satisfied with the caravan?

It was a great success, I say.

Your success, she says.

Our success, I say.

Her fingers caress and probe, working at my tender soles.

Ah, I say.

It hurts?

No, no. Only as it should do.

Was Mohammed Issa asleep? she asks.

Yes, I say. No difference there.

He is getting old, she says.

Issa is no older than I am but I do not point that out. She makes circles with her thumbs, the bony heels of her hands.

What else was discussed? she asks.

This and that, I say. Market rates, the usual things. A problem with the kasava sellers.

Pah, she says dismissively. They are a bunch of Chichimecs.

Abd al-Wahid will issue a complaint, I say. They will be punished. Ah!

Her hands are pressing harder now. But the pain is a good pain.

For a while I lose myself in the sensations of the feet. The feeling is both sharp and dull, like the rhythm of that axe. Reflected sunlight from the bowl plays across the ceiling and the walls, as if across the hull of a ship moored against a quay.

I remember the first time my wife did this for me.

She was not then my wife. We were beside a river. Crossing through the current's pull, I had slipped and cut my foot on a hidden edge of rock. I came limping onto shore with blood welling through my toes.

While my companions waded up, hauling their horses after them, I sat upon a rotten log and Malinala washed my feet. I did not ask her to do this. She did it without comment. First she rinsed away the blood and then she dressed the wound with leaves, green leaves from the riverbank.

The dust and grime of travelling commingled with the water.

Several of the other men laughed and made the usual jokes. I paid them no regard, as I pay them none today.

This must have been a year or more before we entered Mexica. Before we first glimpsed Tenochtitlan from the pass of the Moor's First Sigh.

She was still teaching me to speak.

River, she said in Nahuatl, pointing to the water's flow. Then she said, The tree that weeps, pointing to an uli tree.

She fingered my injured toe.

Blood, she said. Blood.

Eli, she says now, which brings me back to myself. I gaze down at my feet, which gleam with scented oil. They look like idols one might find in the temple of a pampered god, basking in their own soft light. They feel new, as no other part of me feels new.

Nothing else? she asks.

Nothing of what? I say.

She has put away the bowl and is patting my ankles with a cloth.

No more a man of dust, she says. Look, I have brought you something.

Upon my desk in the largest room sits a rough clay bowl. I lift its lid, expecting food. The bowl is full of water.

I took him from the lake, she says.

There stirs a pale, translucent shape. Four tiny hands. A smiling face.

It is a water-god, I say.

Axolotl, she says.

Bringing the bowl towards my face, I take a closer look inside. The water-god swims urgently, gliding off the sides. Its movements are distressed but the smile does not leave its face.

I thought he might amuse you, she says. If not, we can eat him.

Only in the marketplace have I seen these curious beasts before. They are not gods, of course, but neither are they fish. They resemble illustrations I have seen of salamanders, which live in fire and are prized by alchemists. But water-gods live in the lake and are prized by the Mexica.

I have only ever seen them fried, mounded in charred pyramids, a delicacy much enjoyed at festivals and important feasts. Their flavour, I have been told, resembles that of chicken. Neither the Torah nor the Qur'an mentions them, nor creatures like them, so whether God considers them unclean I really do not know. The imam has forbidden them, but that is just the imam.

The creature's flesh is pulpy, smooth, as lucent as my oiled feet. It wears a crown of feathered gills like the headdress of an emperor.

I will keep it as a pet, I say. When I feed it I will think of you.

The water-god looks up at me with a child's purity.

Later, as we lie in bed, my wife tells the story of the Feathered Snake and the underworld.

I used to write these stories down. Now I simply listen.

Before the Fifth Sun dawned, she says, the Feathered Snake went to the place where the underworld meets the earth, and where the earth meets the sky. The Thirteen Heavens stood above and the Nine Hells lay below. He went down into the earth, through the nine layers of death, to recover the bones of mankind and bring them up to the light.

With him went the Dog-Headed God, for the Dog-Headed God is the evening star and knows his way through the dark. They travelled deep into the earth until they reached the deepest place, and there they saw the fleshless face of the Lord of the Dead.

The Lord of the Dead demanded music in exchange for mankind's bones. He gave the Feathered Snake a flute, but the flute had no holes. So the Feathered Snake summoned worms to drill holes in the flute, and he summoned bees to make the sound of music. The Lord of the Dead gave him the bones, but only to borrow, not to keep. For in the end the bones of all things must return to death.

As the gods returned from the underworld the Feathered Snake dropped the bones, which shattered into many parts. That is why all people now are different heights and sizes. But they came safely through the dark, for the Feathered Snake is the morning star and knows his way back to the light.

On the earth, the gods drank smoke and made meal of the bones, she says. They mixed the meal with blood and maiz and shaped it into men. The Fifth Sun dawned. Men walk the earth.

But in the earth the Lord of the Dead is still waiting for his bones.

My wife has told this tale before. It is never the same twice. Sometimes the worms are ants, and the bees are flies or hummingbirds. Sometimes the morning star drops the bones and sometimes he is tricked. Sometimes he falls into a pit. Sometimes a quail startles him.

Do you believe these tales? I ask.

She does not recognise the question.

As my body slackens into sleep, Malinala breathing next to me, I wonder if my bones will be buried here in the New Maghreb. And if they are, will hairless dogs bring them up again?

I wake up later, in the dark, to hear the echoes of their howls.

And far beyond, a stony roar.

It is the mountain speaking.

· TWO ·

I WAS born in the heart of Andalus, in the city of Tulaytulah. They called it the City of Three Cultures. I suppose they call it that today. It lies on a hill above a river that flows past it on three sides. The river is green. The countryside around is planted with olive trees. The city is famous for its steel, and for its mosques and synagogues, and for its churches too, for the caliph's law is honoured there. Many roads start and end in that city. It is far from any sea.

My father was a seller of wool who travelled throughout the caliphate, from the Frankish mountains of the north to the deserts in the south. As a boy I often went with him.

My mother died when I was very young. I did not know her.

When Malinala asks me what I remember of Andalus, I sometimes tell her about the storks who build their nests upon its roofs, piling up sticks year by year.

Either that or the jostling masts in the harbour at Qadis.

Or I try to describe the sound of a hundred calls to prayer issuing from a hundred mouths, each the same but not the same, and how the swallows cut and glide in the air above the minarets, each the same but not the same.

Or the taste of mulberries.

Once, after drinking xocolatl, I found myself telling her of a dusty road in the north. My father and I were leading mules we were not allowed to ride. We passed a village of Christians, their houses slovenly and low, and watched a party of worshippers stoop inside their grey stone church. Before the door had swung closed I heard a bell ring thrice. It was a mysterious sound, rare because the ringing of bells is only permitted within four walls, never in the open air. That is also the caliph's law.

I stared at the church, a box more closed to me than any mosque, and imagined men in golden robes kissing bones by candlelight at the foot of their tall and terrifying cross.

They are dhimmis like us, my father said. But I knew they were not like us.

That is all I remember of that road with my father.

Over the years I have asked Malinala what she remembers of her home, but she does not specify. It was a place of green grass, that is all she says.

From my own research I believe that it was a Nahua-mushrik town some hundred miles south of here. The Mexica caught her people in the Flower War. They sold her to the Mayayans. The Mayayans sold her to us.

We freed her.

I freed her.

That was twenty years ago. We were still trading on the coast, far from this high hinterland, buying precious stones and tortoiseshell, sailing back and forth to the Qarib Sea. There were fewer of us then. We had heard stories of Tenochtitlan but had no means to get here.

I had learned to speak Mayayan but knew nothing of Nahuatl, the language of the Mexica, whose city we desired to see. Malinala, having been a slave, had knowledge of both tongues. We were two links in a chain, connecting one thing to the next. Arabic to Mayayan. Mayayan to Nahuatl. Nahuatl to Arabic.

I freed her.

She freed us.

There is another memory that I have never shared with her. One I keep close to myself. Again it is of my father. In the green north-west of Andalus, where it often rains, and there are hills and apple trees, there was a peninsula that the Christians called World's End. In those ignorant days it was believed that there was nothing west of there, only the endless rolling waves stretching into nothingness. It was the first time I had ever seen the Sea of Darkness. We led our mules along that coast, on our way from one place to the next, and when the rain clouds blew away we watched the sun go down.

There are tales, my father said as the two of us squinted west, tales of magic islands there. Of lands beyond the setting sun.

Do men like us live there? I asked.

He laughed. They are only stories.

An aching feeling came to me, something that I could not name. I felt breathless and unmoored, as if I were somehow falling. The wind was blustering from the west and it stirred my father's hair. My father led the mules on but the dazzling vision held me.

The blazing orb of light went down, turning the Sea of Darkness gold. I watched as it touched the waves and a shining pathway opened. It seemed a passage that might be walked, a golden road into the west, the distant country of the sun.

Come now, my father said. There is nothing out there.

We turned away from the darkened sea and from the last spark of the sun. Rain washed over us again. We crept through mud and darkness. But it never left my mind, that golden road across the waves. That dream.

I have not yet woken.

Early in the morning I go to check the water-god.

Malinala is not in bed, but the bed still holds her shape.

As I cross the room I am surprised to find that my body is aroused. The warm familiarity of the sensation makes it strange. It is like meeting an old friend with whom I once shared a confidence, with whom I was intimate in my youth but have not thought about for some time.

We acknowledge each other respectfully but go our separate ways.

Malinala has laid out fruit, shrivelled dates and maizcake. The morning's xocolatl beans sit ready in the pan.

I go to my desk and lift the lid of the clay bowl. The water-god, the axolotl, lies beneath the water. At first

I think it might be dead, for it does not move at all, but when I give the bowl a swirl it wags its pale hands. A single bubble rises up. Its lipless mouth is smiling. I take a piece of the fruit and drop it into the bowl. The creature does not react.

I put on my ordinary robe and go to the door. A mushrik lad is loitering out there, as a mushrik lad often is. Peace be with you, I say.

He puts his hand upon his heart, the way he has been taught.

Fetch me some worms, I say. I will give you tasty dates.

His bare feet slap the stones of the courtyard as he goes. He runs in an ungainly lope, his arms hanging at his sides. There are marks upon his back. I squint but cannot make them out.

An importer of silk from Ishbiliyya is drinking tea on his step, perched cross-legged in the shade, and raises his hand to say hello. I greet him back, then step inside to perform my ablutions.

After I have breakfasted, watching the light grow hot outside, I sit down at my desk and take a sheet of paper. I draw two circles on it, one coloured black and one left white, along with a seven-branched tree.

Then I decide to leave the task for some other moment.

Instead of continuing with the missive to the emperor, as Abd al-Wahid asked of me, I open the codex I am currently translating. This particular set of glyphs relates the history of the Seven Caves, when seven tribes emerged from seven rocky wombs in the north and made their way to the south. The Mexica were favoured by the Left-Handed

Hummingbird. They warred upon the other tribes and killed them or made slaves of them. For a time they stayed in Aztlan, the Place of the White-Feathered Heron.

Their god then led them further south through the land of thorns and the land of stones, driving out the other tribes and scattering them from their cities. He was the strongest god, the god of war and the sun, and they were his chosen people. That was in the year 1 Knife.

But I do not wish to work today. The glyphs give me a headache.

Presently the boy returns with a fistful of grey worms. I do not ask where he got them from. Presumably from the lakeside. I give him dates in return, from the ones Malinala left for me, and send him on his way.

The marks upon his back are welts, as from a beating.

At least, I hope they are welts. They resemble, passingly, other marks that I have seen.

I drop the worms into the bowl and leave them to the water-god.

When I step outside again the air is the temperature of blood. The Moorish Quarter is still calm. Beyond the gate, the chosen people go about their business.

The flaming sun is seeping over the flat roofs of Tenochtitlan. Blue smoke threads from cooking fires, black smoke from the temples. The sky holds a single cloud, caught in a smudge above the lake. A bird hangs in the clear air. Perhaps it is an eagle.

No guard stands at the gate today. He might have overslept. He might have indulged in cactus wine and become intoxicated, although that is not allowed. The fact that it is not allowed does not mean it does not happen. There was a time when the Caliph's Gate was manned by brightly armoured men with arquebuses in their hands, and I am glad that time has passed.

The ripples roll across the lake. This is a time of peace.

I walk beneath the archway, over the green-flecked cobblestones, where no scimitar is raised or lowered to mark my passing. Mohammed Issa is conversing with two respected merchants there. I know them from the market-place, dealers in feathers and jaguar skins, though I do not know their names. Their lower lips are plugged with jade. They wear their hair in topknots. Both wear sleek white cloaks, one hemmed in crimson, one in blue. Neither of them has a beard, for mushriks seldom do.

Peace be with you, Issa says.

And with you, I say. How do you live? I ask the merchants.

We live well, they say.

Good sun, I say.

Good sun, they reply.

We are going to the House of the Reed, says Issa. Will you walk with us?

I tell them it is my way too, although in reality I have no destination.

We walk together along the road, the white-cloaked pair in front of us. Occasionally they stop to exchange pleas-antries with their fellows. I have always been impressed by the courtesy the Mexica show in their dealings with one another, the rituals of their hierarchy. Moorish manners at their best can sometimes match this gracefulness. At their worst they cast us in the same light as Chichimecs.

The Mexica of Tenochtitlan despise these artless Chichimecs, who wander the bare lands of the north. They do not cultivate maiz and build no cities of their own. When we first came to this valley, wanderers as we were, there were some who called us that.

If anyone calls us that today, it is not within our earshot.

Issa takes me by the arm and speaks in his soft, considered way. So, he says, I am wondering, what did you think of yesterday?

I think you were asleep, I say.

He laughs in three successive rasps, like the throaty calling of a bird. I may have briefly closed my eyes, he says. The days these days are long.

I think the beverages were poor, I say. He rasps twice this time.

Does the news not worry you? he asks, further down the road.

Lots of things worry me, I say. The huracan-wind of the Qarib Sea. The feuding of the Mayayans. Frankish pirates. Camel-pox.

But about this Benmessaoud, he says, who is coming or not coming.

I do not know, I say. Not yet, anyway. We do not know what he wants.

Maybe not, he says. But we know what he does not like.

Good sun, one of the merchants calls, genuflecting at a man who is beating the air with a feather fan.

Good sun, the man replies. His face is marked with blue tattoos. The feathers waggle like a broken wing attempting flight.

He does not like tubaq, I say. He does not like xocolatl.

He does not like you, Eli.

But he does not know me.

Nevertheless, Issa says. The point is theoretical.

He might not like you either, I say.

No rasps this time.

Issa has a face that is deeply scored by the sun, creased into a latticework of lines across his cheeks and brow. He has a white tuft for a beard. His eyes are slow and green. Once he was a carpenter, and his large, knotted hands still bear the saw-scars of that trade. He made his wealth in ceiba wood, which is prized for its straight grain.

He was also married once, to a Taiyno woman from Qubah. She was the daughter of a chief. I believe he was in love. But it only endured for a couple of years, and then she went back to her people. There were rumours of a child, but it is not talked about.

How is your wife? Issa asks, as if our thoughts were linked somehow. You must pass her my regards.

I will do that, I say.

She was of great service to me several weeks ago, he says. Did she mention it to you?

I do not recall it, I say.

I wished to buy a huehxolotl-bird from the Street of Fowl, he says, but the seller would not sell to me. One of those suspicious peasants from the far side of the lake.

Malinala was nearby. She spoke to him on my behalf. He sold the bird immediately.

She has that effect, I say.

She is clever, Issa says.

Indeed she is, I say.

She always was clever, he says.

How was the bird? I ask.

These juicy huehxolotl-birds are waddling, unsightly things with livid crimson heads that look as if they have been boiled. Their roasted flesh is flavoursome.

It was excellent, he says. Though perhaps not worth all that I paid.

Why would he not sell to you?

I do not know. He was ignorant. Malinala put him in his place.

Well, I am glad of it, I say.

We walk on in silence.

By the wharf of the grand canal smooth-chested men in kanoas are unloading nets of fish. Women with baskets on their heads jostle in the crowd. Two hairless dogs skulk beneath a ruined wall, one with yellow skin, one blue, both with wagging purple tongues, looking on with hungry eyes. A woman throws a stone towards them but they do not react.

What business do you have at the House of the Reed? I ask as we draw near that place.

I am making a contract with these men to export jaguar skins, he says. God willing it will be lucrative. We are meeting the emperor's notaries there to formalise the particulars.

At the mention of the emperor a silence opens up again. It is an empty, waiting space. Moctezuma and my wife, both mentioned, float there in the air. But, like the hairless dogs, neither of us makes a move.

It reminds me of the younger man's urge that came to me earlier. A thing to be taken notice of, then tucked back in its place.

Ahead lies the House of the Reed, a high stone building with white walls and steps ascending to its door. By the door sits an eagle knight in his suit of feathers.

With peace, my friend, Issa says, squeezing the soft flesh of my arm. Wish your wife good health from me.

I place my hand upon my heart. Until the next sun, I say to the impassive white-cloaked men.

Until the next sun, they say. They place their hands upon their hearts and we go our separate ways.

From which direction would he come? This is what I ask myself.

I am standing on the shore looking back towards the city.

From which direction would he come, if, indeed, he were to come?

All roads lead to Mexica, Abd al-Wahid said.

When I do not know where to go I come to where the marshes start. When I do not know where to go, and when I want privacy. Privacy is a commodity rarer than gold in Tenochtitlan, and, to me, more valuable. I have walked the floating road that leads west from the city.

It is the shortest of the roads and in truth it does not float, as none of the roads really float, but rests upon wooden pilings sunk into the lakebed. Upon connecting with the shore it branches, running west and south. But there are smaller pathways sneaking through the reeds. They might be made by fishermen or fowlers, or by animals. Or by people hunting water-gods. Perhaps my wife came here. The pathway I have taken now runs between two grey lagoons to my favourite vantage point, where there is water all around. Its mirrored surface holds the sky.

I look back towards the island on which stands the city.

Its rooftops are just visible beyond the swaying beds of reeds, shifting in and out of sight. Taller, and more significant, stand the summits of the temples. From here they look like distant peaks in a range that I will never reach, a place that might be seen in dreams. Or in memories.

Sunlight boils off the lake and the buildings wobble in the haze. When I blink they disappear, then swim back into focus. The city and all that it contains might simply be smudged away, like a smear upon a windowpane. These squalid marshes would return to a time before all cities.

According to the codices, the ragged tribe of the Mexica came to this valley as wanderers, dispossessed and displaced, having struggled through the wilderness. Here, the strongest of the gods favoured them with a sign. On an island in the lake the Left-Handed Hummingbird placed an eagle on a cactus with a snake grasped in its claws. They built their city on that spot. This was their promised land.

That history was revealed to me not by the translated glyphs, or from Malinala's lips, but from the mouth of

Moctezuma. We were drinking cactus wine. In return I told him of the portent of the burning bush, and the wandering of the Israelites, and of our own promised land.

Why did you not stay there? he asked. I did not attempt an answer.

Something tingles on my neck and I slap the pain away. I lift my palm to reveal splattered insect parts. This place is rife with biting flies. I wipe the mess upon my robe. From a phial I daub my skin with lemon-scented oil.

The mushriks of the Qarib Sea repelled the insects of those isles with the pungent grease of crocodiles. It had an effective stench.

But there are no crocodiles in this promised land.

An eagle throttling a snake. The temples wafting through the reeds. Bits of time keep floating past in this place where land and water meet. This happens more and more these days, as I look back through the years.

But I have come to this place to look towards the future.

From which direction will he come, this Benmessaoud? When he comes. With his men of God, whom the caliph must be happy to be rid of. From the bag at my side I take my Frankish spyglass. It is a wonderful device, about the length of half my arm, which I bought at much expense for the journey towards Mexica.

Through its lens, now smeared with age, I first glimpsed Tenochtitlan.

I put the small end to my eye and sweep the wide circumference. Reeds. Reeds. Low purple hills. The outlined smoking mountain. It is not smoking now but clean, like a mouth that has been wiped. Mountains. Mountains. Hills. More reeds. Then, again, the staggered tidy rooftops of the city. The greatest of the pyramids is crowned with two trapezoid shrines. One has crimson walls, one blue. One for sun, one rain.

Lazy specks circle above, but I can see no people there.

I scan the view from east to north, north to south, south to east. The world swims in a lucent disc. The horizon trembles. The obvious angle of approach is across the Moor's First Sigh, the natural passage from the coast, with the smoking mountain to the south. The Tlaxcalans might point him this way, as Abd al-Wahid suggested. Enemies of the Mexica, who fear them and resent them and in many ways resemble them, they might even march with him to settle ancient rivalries.

Or will he come from further south through the farmlands of the Nahua, Malinala's countrymen, who hate this city equally? Or from the north? I doubt the north. West? It might be possible.

All roads lead to Mexica. But there are many roads.

There is a scrabbling in my hair. I pull away a horrid mite, all legs and wings, and stamp it dead. It leaves behind a smear of blood. Mine or someone else's.

The scent of lemons does not suffice. My arms are stippled with red dots. It must be the season when these marsh-flies breed prodigiously, spawning in the stagnant ponds. I cannot remain here long or I will be eaten.

A splash, and dimly through the reeds a kanoa glides by, paddled by a fisherman with bowl-shaped hair. Probably not from Tenochtitlan, but from one of the villages that pays tribute to the city. I hold my breath and wait. Oily ripples lap the reeds. The vessel passes noiselessly and the fellow does not see me.

That is the thing about this place. Even here I am not alone. There is never privacy.

The flies are everywhere.

I wipe the lens of the spyglass with its little velvet cloth and put the instrument away. It has not seen anything.

Following the buzzing path, I retreat to the floating road.

A common dish of Tenochtitlan is maiz-cakes of spicy dough steamed inside a husk of leaves, served with red tomatl-fruit. From a stall I purchase three. One for myself, one for my wife and one for charity.

A hairless dog grins as I eat, tracking each morsel with its eyes, but I have no charity to offer to its species.

In a small public square a man is lying on his back, knees bent against his chest, with a heavy log between his toes. He scowls with concentration. In a violent motion he hurls the log into the air and catches it as it falls, only to hurl it up again, spinning it end on end, now balancing it on one toe and tipping it to make it fall, catching it with his other foot and hurling it back up again. A vapid child next to him warbles on a flute.

Is this some sort of punishment? I ask the woman who prepared my food.

It is entertainment, she replies, staring at me blankly.

I meant it as a joke, of course, but they seldom get my jokes.

The Mexica laugh frequently, like children, at all kinds of things. Their jokes are physical, corporeal, often carnal. I have seen them laugh at rain, and at costumed dancers as they gurn, and at public accidents, and at people being flayed. The imam says that he hears the voice of devils when they laugh. But I doubt the imam has laughed in thirty years.

At last the log thumps to the ground and the sweating man lies back. Bystanders make offerings. The child puts down his flute. I consider giving them my spare maiz-cake, this hapless pair, and start to cross the square. But I am intercepted.

A mushrik woman blocks my path. Lord of strangers, she says.

She has a baby in her arms, wrapped tightly in a grubby rag. From her unembroidered hem I know that she is of low caste, and also from her jewellery, which is only wood and bone. Her eyes, though, have a fierce light, burning like a horse's.

Will you come with me? she asks. She stares at me with urgency.

Where? I ask, gulping the maiz.

My child is sick. My little girl, she says.

I am no healer.

From across the water, she says.

What? I ask.

Like you, she says. From over there. From far away.

I do not understand, I say.

My lord, she attempts again. Her lips are trembling. I doubt that she has ever spoken to a Moorish man before.

It is unusual, certainly, for a woman like her to speak to me, or indeed a woman of any rank. Unbefitting. Out of place. That is why my wife's behaviour causes consternation.

One of the reasons, anyway.

The woman grabs my sleeve.

I gently pull my arm away, but people are beginning to stare and pass judgement in the crowd. I do not wish to cause a scene. And so I let myself be led, still clutching those two steaming husks, across the square and into the streets that run behind it. The woman goes ahead of me, glancing back frequently to check that I am following. We skirt an empty marketplace and cross a ditch of sewage. We reach a narrow neighbourhood that I have never seen before, having had no cause to come. The houses here are not of stone but mud, with wattled walls. Their roofs are conical and thatched. Ducks splash in puddled yards. There is an acrid, smoky smell that becomes more pronounced as I follow her stooping form below the lintel of a door, entering a darkened room that is packed with bodies. It reeks of burning herbs and sweat, and of something bittersweet. Bodies block the door behind. The air is foetid, heavy.

Here, she says. Please, my lord.

There are hands upon my arms and a murmur in the room. I cannot see anything. Blind, I am nudged forwards. The only meagre points of light are a few splints of pine burning with a sallow glow, soaked in their own resinous oil. There is something on the floor. Twisted sheets. A body.

Someone holds up a flame. Before me lies the little girl from the nest of ants.

49

Her mouth is open, her eyes closed. She gleams like something lacquered. The pink and purple blotches have multiplied and spread, patterning her body. For a moment I imagine that the ants have crawled inside, have built their mazes in her skin, and these livid bumps are their points of excavation. But of course it is not ants.

She is stricken, says the woman.

The angry voice of a man commences shouting in the room. His accent is unrefined, unlike the subtle dialect of the city's noblemen, its priesthood or its merchant class, and I catch but a few words. Why is this stranger here? he shouts. And then a string of consonants. Other mushriks remonstrate and strong hands guide him from the room. Behind the wall he rages on. A duck erupts in outraged squawks. I imagine he has kicked it.

Help her, the woman pleads, as if nothing has occurred.

Lady, I do not know how.

We have tried everything, she says.

I am no healer, I say again. No physician, just a man of trade. Have you not asked your priests?

We have asked the gods, she says.

She gestures across the bed to a smoky household shrine. Two idols crouch there, one female and one male. The female, I believe, is the Goddess of Bright Sweat, the male the Lord of the Root, both deities of medicine, but their forms are indistinct. They are grubbed with a residue of amaranth, ash and blood.

Our gods cannot help, she says. They do not know this sickness because it is from far away. You are from far away.

What can I do? I say.

The God of Strangers, she says.

A mutter fills the room.

Please, my lord. Will you speak with him? The Faceless God. He might know.

Well, I can pray, I say.

They say that he is very strong.

Dumbly I nod.

She is grabbing at my arm again. I can hardly breathe from fumes, some smouldering decoction. The little girl opens her eyes, a flash of white, and slides them shut.

Yes, I say, I will ask Him. Now I must go. But I will ask.

I am seized with sudden fear that the girl will open her eyes again and see me, and remember me. A bearded, foreign face staring down as she robbed an ants' nest. I do not know why it frightens me, this thought, but I back away. There are hands all over me, patting and cajoling.

Hearing commotion in the room, the girl makes a bleating sound as I struggle through the hands. I do not look at her.

Until the next sun, I say, but still they will not let me go. They are trying to give me things. Useless things. Beads, and bits of twine, and crudely fashioned likenesses lumped from maiz or from clay, and other votive clutter. A knot of hair, perhaps the girl's. A fistful of black seeds.

I am clutching two maiz-cakes, no longer hot, in my hand, and as I stumble to the yard one of them slops into the mud. A purple duck examines it. I hurriedly retreat.

The shouting man scowls at me from the shade of a slatted wall, but he is not shouting now and is too shy to speak. Minutes later I am back in the public square. The superstitious offerings I conceal in my bag, not knowing what else to do with them. The third maiz-cake I eat, in hasty secret gulps. My wife will have to do without.

I think about the ants' nest and the stolen eggs.

I walk through the city I know so well, that I do not know at all. The incident has shaken me. It does not presage well. I must speak to Abd al-Wahid, but first I must arrange my visit to the emperor, but first I must inform Malinala that she may not come. That the merchants do not want her there. I do not know what she will say.

I should have kept that maiz-cake.

My route home takes me past the pitted wall of yellow stone that marks the western boundary of the temple quarter. A priest of the Smoking Mirror is passing down the road, a shining black obsidian disc, his instrument of prophecy, gleaming upon his chest. His head is shaved to the scalp and his eyes are smudged with ashes. I consider giving him the offerings, but he avoids looking at me. That is another wall.

There is no activity today in the great temple square, into which at festivals tens of thousands teem. Through an open entranceway I glimpse the level space beyond. Acres of blank stone stretch to the distant temple steps, at the foot of which a few dark figures congregate. I cannot make them out from here. Closer, but still far away, stands the Rack of Skulls. Its cargo shines in the sun, whiter near the top and yellower as they descend, stacked like desiccating gourds. There must be several hundred there. They hold little interest for me.

When I first came to this place I could hardly look away. Like the rest, I walked about with my mouth hanging open. We had not seen such things before. The bloody ears of the priests, lacerated ritually. The heaps of slender ivory that were revealed, upon inspection, to be thigh bones, long and clean. Back in Andalus, of course, we had seen men beheaded, in the usual way of things, and some of us had been in wars, or at least in skirmishes. But none of us had seen a man impale his penis with a lance and laugh to see the blood run out. To please the gods. To feed the sun.

The sun blazes at me now. It does not appear ill-fed.

The weaker of my countrymen were horrified or outraged. I was merely curious. I was practical. We had come here to trade, to stitch the land with caravans and send ships across the sea, to thread together Tenochtitlan with our distant caliphate. Neither horror nor outrage could be said to serve our purpose.

After twenty years here I have grown so used to things that I do not see them any more. Or I do not remember how I felt when they were new. When my tired eyes were new. It is like remembering a time of only white and grey, before I knew what crimson was, or the colour of sunlight on the lake.

Before I was who I am. Before I met Malinala.

Turning the corner of the road at the southern end of the temple wall, I do remember one thing that comes with sudden clarity. In the Moorish Quarter's early days, before the mosque had been built, I was walking near this place when I saw a drop of blood. Further on, another drop. Another, then another. Every time I thought I had lost the trail, there was another drop. I wondered if I was being led to wonders, or to death. At length, in a cobbled alleyway, I overtook a small boy who was carrying a bowl, cupping it with both his arms as if it were a pail of milk, attempting to step carefully. He was unsteady on his feet with the liquid weight inside. Every time he stumbled a drop of bright blood splashed out. I followed him until he turned through the doorway of a temple.

That was when I understood that I would never know this place. It was also, strangely, when I first thought of it as home.

A group of mushrik converts is departing through the Caliph's Gate as I arrive just after noon. There cannot be more than twenty-five or thirty in the city. Peace be with you, I say, but my salutation is met with the usual depthless stares. They are dressed in unadorned white robes and simple skullcaps.

They go past in single file glancing at me one by one. They are like a line of ducks heading towards a pond. Most speak no Arabic beyond the sounds they repeat in prayers, hardly knowing what they mean. Some of them have strings of prayer beads wrapped around their fingers. They have learned to face towards Makkah, a place that is incomprehensible to them, and bend their knees a certain way and touch their foreheads to the earth. Sometimes I suspect they are still bowing towards the sun.

Most Moors call them mushriks still, but the term is paradoxical. Mushriks worship many gods. They pray to rivers, rocks and rain. They are idolators, like the Jews who once worshipped the Golden Calf. When a mushrik proclaims that there is no god but God, he is not a mushrik any more.

But habits of speech, as well as those of mind, are hard to break.

These Mexica Muslims do not know what to make of me. They know that I am set apart but they do not know why. They know that we venerate different books but the stories in them are the same. My god, like theirs, is the One God, the God of Many Names. And yet He is something else. I am something else. The difference between a Muslim and a Jew, to the unschooled Mexica, is as subtle and as slight as the difference, to the unschooled Moor, between a Mexica and a Mayayan, or a Tlaxcalan and a Zapotec. My rank is both high and low to them. Perhaps this explains their wariness.

This, and the knowledge of whom I share my bed with.

The greater mass of Tenochtitlan regards them as an oddity, as far as I can ascertain. There is no persecution, no charge of apostasy. Between acceptance and disinterest there is peace, for now at least. And for now that is enough.

It has to be enough.

From my conversations with Moctezuma, who takes an interest in such things, I know that he considers God to be an incarnation of the Feathered Snake, the Smoking Mirror or the Left-Handed Hummingbird, depending on the time of day. I have not told the imam this. The poor man has enough to deal with.

One of the passing converts whispers something to the man behind. I imagine it relates to me, but I do not catch the words. The prayer beads rattle through his fingers, going round and round and round. Each bead represents one of the ninety-nine names of God.

As the converts disperse into the streets, they remove their skullcaps.

The mosque attendant is at work sweeping the courtyard with a broom, rolling back small waves of dust. He is whistling a tune. At first I cannot place its jerky, jaunty melody, which is familiar and yet strange, then I recognise it as a song the mushriks play. I heard it not an hour ago, played on a child's flute.

That is a pretty tune, I say.

He stops whistling at once.

Do you think that I might enter? I say on an impulse.

He shrugs uncertainly, extending his arm towards the door.

A thousand thanks, I say.

He shrugs again, scratches his eye and goes back to his sweeping.

My shoes are the only shoes left outside the door. The mosque is empty. The imam, at this time, will be at lunch. I walk into the tiled space and smell its cool, familiar smell, part dusty and part sweet. The carpet is rough beneath my toes. Light creeps through coloured glass. Above me is the air-filled dome, the lamps hanging on their chains, before me is the gold-patterned niche that indicates the east, that points the way towards my home, which is no longer home.

On the far side of the wall lies the smaller synagogue. That is where I should go to pray, in accordance with the caliph's law. To light the seven candles of the menorah the Mayayans made for me. To yearn towards Jerusalem rather than towards Makkah. Both of those distant cities, neither of which I have ever seen, or dreamed of visiting, are as indistinct as the smoke above the candle flames. Jerusalem is not real to me.

Tenochtitlan is real.

When the rabbi was alive I went to synagogue each week. We would drink cactus wine and eat challah bread made from maiz. He had studied in Tulaytulah, the city in which I was born, and he missed it more than me, with a painful urgency. He was always pining to return. I liked his company. He was a younger man than me, but he died of fever-sweats almost seven years ago and has never been replaced.

There are no other Jews in Mexica, perhaps none in the New Maghreb.

I should go to pray there now, but the space feels much too small for me. Instead I stand here in the mosque, where the space feels much too large. I close my eyes and listen to the passing sounds in the street outside, the hawkers' cries, the distant hum.

I feel the emptiness of the dome above me.

The mother of the stricken girl wishes me to speak to God, Whom she calls the Faceless God. To ask Him if He knows about the sickness from beyond the sea.

Lord, I say inside my head, but the prayer does not come.

It is hard to fix things down. I cannot see the girl's poxed face. I cannot see her suffering.

Lord, I say. My name is Eli Ben Abram.

But behind my eyes are butterflies, birds wheeling high above the lake.

I think about the volume of air trapped inside this dome, an inverse shape. A negative.

I think about the smoke waiting inside the mountain.

Peace, my Lord, I say.

I cannot pray for more than that.

My knees crack loudly as I stand. I am getting old.

Halfway towards the door, I reach into my bag and touch the offerings. My fingers close around the lump of hair, which I lift into the light. A black, greasy, tangled thing that looks animal. On a whim I stoop, lift the carpet's hem and gently tuck it underneath. I smooth the carpet over it and go towards the door.

I remember when the emperor's men first came to see what we had built, the tiled dome we had raised above what had been four walls, on the land he had granted us when we made our trade agreement. Moctezuma did not come, but he sent his viziers. They wore quetzal-feather cloaks, gold torcs and tall plumed headpieces. They left their footwear at the door as the imam asked of them. They stood here for the longest time, staring politely at the walls and the infinitely repeating tiles and the coloured light falling through the dome. None of them said anything. They were humble and embarrassed.

Where is the god? one asked at last. There is no one here.

· THREE ·

I ɴ the beginning was nothing, she says.
She is combing her dense hair.

And then there was something, I say.

No, she says. Two things.

I have heard this tale before, as I have her other tales.
But I like to fantasise that I am hearing it for the first
time. That my ears are new, as my eyes were once new.

As everything was once new.

The comb drags smoothly through her hair. I crack a
sunflower seed.

From nothing came two things, she says. The Lord of
Duality and the Lady of Duality, who were two and yet
one, one thing and yet two.

Ah, I say, that cannot be. One is one. Two is two.

You are wrong, she says.

Many of my countrymen would raise their eyebrows,
or their fists, at a woman who spoke to them this way. A
mushrik woman at that. I raise the corners of my lips.

Excuse my interruption.

These gods who were two but one made love, she says, like writhing snakes, and from their womb came four more gods. Of east, west, north and south. In the place where all things meet they created the Thirteen Heavens above and the Nine Hells below, with gods to rule in each domain. In between, they stretched a slender crust they called the world.

Outside our room, the grainy evening light is dipping into dusk. A donkey is braying somewhere, hideously and strenuously. Someone laughs not far away, and from the sound I cannot tell if they are Moor or Mexica. Bats dither in the twilight.

The gods began to populate the world with solid things, she says. But every time something was made, it disappeared. Mountains. They disappeared. A waterfall. It disappeared. Everything became nothing. The gods were in confusion. They went to see what was going wrong, and they found that the world they had made was not the world at all but a beast with foaming jaws at each joint of her body, a beast whose hunger would not end, devouring everything. Light, she ate. Dark, she ate. She would not be satisfied.

Like my water-god, I say.

What? she says, frowning.

He has been eating worms, I say.

The comb-scrape halts. Continues.

Hungrier, she says. As if the universe were worms. Do not interrupt me now. I am trying to tell you something.

I crack another sunflower seed. I am listening, I say.

The first four gods approached, she says. First came the Smoking Mirror. He tore his foot from his leg and used its flesh to bait the beast, waving it in front of her. She started to devour it. As she ate, the other gods attacked her from all sides, tearing her into parts. They ripped her into pieces. They used her body to make the earth, her blood to make the lakes and seas, and her bones to make the hills. So the world was made from death.

But everything was dark, she says, for the beast had eaten all the light. So the Smoking Mirror burst into flames to become the sun. But he was only half a sun, because he only had one foot. He dragged himself across the sky, spilling his half-light.

Light such as this, she says, gesturing through the open door. Weak light. One-legged light. Neither one thing nor the other. The brother of the crippled sun, the Feathered Snake, was ashamed. He dragged his brother from the sky and the world was filled with darkness. That was the end of the First Sun.

As if in afterthought she says, And all the men who walked the earth were eaten by jaguars.

Where was it that you learned these tales? I ask, when it is clear that she is done and I will not be reprimanded for my intervention.

Everyone knows them, she says. She puts aside the comb.

Did your parents teach them to you? I ask. Your mother, perhaps?

She glances at me scornfully. She will not be drawn. In all the years that we have shared, she has never spoken of her girlhood, of the life she lived before she was seized in war. Of what she suffered as a slave. There are many things I have not asked.

They are better not to know.

I crack another sunflower seed and roll its kernel with my tongue. It does not taste of anything. Yet I crack another.

Malinala reaches for the brass-handled mirror she keeps, a gift I gave her early in our marriage. She turns it from side to side but does not look into it. Its face reflects the failing light.

I remember her delight when she first received this thing, which I had brought from Andalus. Her people do not know glass. Their mirrors are of obsidian. They call these black reflecting discs smoking mirrors, like the god who is the lord of prophecy.

Our reflections, then, are silver-bright while theirs are dark.

My wife's hair hangs thick and loose, released from its complicated plaits. It runs the length of her back down almost to her knees. Its volume amazes me, as does its economy when it is tightly coiled in the elaborate style she has, a knotwork of her own design. In the marketplace I have heard her called the Woman of the Knots.

Also the Woman of Two Tongues. No doubt there are other names.

As she picks up the comb and starts to pull from its teeth the strands of hair that have been caught, throwing them carelessly to the floor, I am reminded of the lock of hair beneath the carpet. Why did I leave it there? The act was inexplicable. What if the imam should find it there, or the mosque attendant? I imagine the bare feet of my friends and countrymen pressing down on it, their foreheads almost touching it. It makes me faintly nauseous.

My wife glances at the shiny glass then turns away.

My mouth is full of sunflower seeds whose shells I have cracked absently, without being aware of it. I chew them rhythmically but my mouth forgets to swallow. Like a camel chewing grain, Malinala says, watching me.

Now it is my turn to scowl.

My ugly deer, she says.

And then she smiles, which brings happiness to my heart. I rest my arm upon her knee.

Where will they be now? she asks, and I know that in her mind is an image of the caravan dragging out across the land, the camels striding patiently, their faces turned towards the sea. The baggage swaying on their backs, marked with the sigil of my house.

Through the mountains now, I say. Past Tlaxcala, anyway. If their road has been fair they might be crossing the brown plains.

Three weeks until the sea? she asks.

Three weeks until the sea.

And now the image in my mind is of our little trading post, the harbour in the sandy bay, a place I have not seen for years. The settlement will be larger now. I can see its busy quay. Officials of the caliphate who have never ventured more than a mile into the hinterland are waiting there expectantly, eyes turned towards the west. A fleet of anchored merchant ships rides gently on the waves.

Then, as if it has been stung, I lift my arm from my wife's knee. What if among those vessels now lie Benmessaoud's?

Is something wrong? asks my wife.

No, I think, the Mayayans said that he sailed further north. Unless we have been misinformed.

Nothing is wrong, I say.

She turns the mirror idly and I see one half of her face, one eye, one corner of her mouth. The reflection flashes out at me.

Whatever has alarmed you, she says, you need not worry. Chew your seeds, my ugly deer. No more stories for tonight.

My mirrored face looks back at her. It is time for bed, I say.

I walk into the other room, pulling my shirt over my head.

And all the men who walked the earth were eaten by jaguars.

In the morning she is gone again. Always she is gone.

Are you content for your wife to roam the streets in such a way? other men have sometimes asked.

No, I would like to say.

Yet somehow I am happy.

This might seem to some a perplexing thing to say. Can one be happy and not content? Where is the line between the two?

In my own life, that line has been the Sea of Darkness.

In Andalus I might have been content, as my father was content. I might have traded wool like him, hauling mules down dusty lanes, bargaining with Riffish shepherds in the mountains of the south. Sleeping in caravanserais. Bowing to soldiers on the road, half fearful and half reassured. Content to remain a dhimmi, a protected person but contained, as all protected people are.

I did not know happiness until I took that blazing road. I did not know happiness until I came to the New Maghreb.

I did not know it was happiness then. I did not know what it was. But neither did I know, nor did any of us know, that it was the New Maghreb. We thought it was the Indies.

I did not know it was happiness because it felt like other things. It felt like fear, bewilderment, privation and often sickness. The early days were very hard. I witnessed men around me die. I felt responsible for their deaths because I had brought them to this place, had led them here across the sea, with those papers in my hand and no idea what I had done, what futures I had opened up. It did not feel like happiness and takes the forms, now I look back, of fragmented images that occasionally dazzle out at me with an intensity that is shocking, like my wife's face in the mirror. The bone whiteness of a beach. Unexpected purple hills. The ears of my chestnut horse pricked towards a mountain range. The mountains fearsome, bright with snow.

Our journey through the Moor's First Sigh.

The first time I looked down to see Tenochtitlan.

Surely that was happiness then, the purest I have known. We had struggled through the pass, our faces numb with cold. Our horses' breaths smoked in the light. For days we had hardly eaten. Our Tlaxcalan guides led on, and even then we did not know if our trust in them would be betrayed or if some ambush lay ahead amidst the wastes of scattered rock. Reeling from the altitude, we were almost too tired to care.

And then the pass came to an end and this valley lay below. In the valley was a lake. On the lake, a city.

There it is, the Tlaxcalans said. The City of the Mexica.

One Tlaxcalan raised his club. Another mouthed a prayer.

I raised the spyglass to my eye but my hand was trembling. The pyramids. The broad canals. The gridded maze of stone-walled streets. It all swam confusingly. Malinala held my hand to keep the vision steady.

Already a legend has been made. It is told in Andalus that one of us, Abd al-Wahid perhaps, uttered a sigh of wonderment as he looked upon this fantasy, like something from a marvellous dream, and ever since then that barren pass has been called the Moor's First Sigh.

If any of us sighed that day, in truth, it was from exhaustion.

I sigh deeply now. It feels good, so I sigh again.

I did not sleep well.

How fares the water-god?

It loiters, snake-like, in its bowl, its crown of gills about its head. The water is no longer clean, polluted by its droppings. Its eyes seem dead. Its mouth still smiles, but I do not think that happiness. Perhaps, in its way, it is content.

Confined and yet protected.

How are you, little dhimmi? I ask. The notion makes me chuckle.

I give the bowl a gentle shake. The water-god gestures at me feebly.

On a whim I scoop it up and place it on my desk. Why would it have feet if it cannot live in air? It takes a step, another step. Its tail drags behind. That delicate, translucent skin, like the pulp of fruit beneath the rind. Its gills hang limply from its head, water streaming off them. I watch as the outlandish newt picks its way, step after step, to an open codex I have not completed work on yet, the glyphs transcribed but not translated, the history of some ancient warfare in the year 12 Rabbit. It hauls itself onto the page, casting its pale face around. What can it be searching for?

The little dhimmi of the lake. Smiling, always smiling.

It will die, says Malinala, standing in the doorway.

The appearance startles me. I did not hear her approach.

Her basket holds fruit, bread, maiz. She must have been to the marketplace.

It needs water like a fish, she says, kicking off her sandals. In the air it will die.

I did not realise that, I say.

Do you wish to watch it drown?

I do not, I say.

Its body struggles weakly as I lift it from the page and replace it in the bowl. Once back in its element it paddles gratefully. A single bubble rises. The gills fan back around its head.

It is happy now, I say.

With the corner of my handkerchief I wipe away the water drops. The page is damp, but the axolotl has done no lasting damage. I peruse the glyphs with a dim, uneasy guilt, aware that I have lately let my self-appointed duties lapse and that the task ahead is long, translating into Arabic the history of the Mexica. The glyphs stare back at me, reluctant to reveal themselves. One day, it is my hope that these completed codices might grace the shelves of the Great Library in Qurtubah.

But not today. My mind is full. The night-time did not bring me rest.

What gossip on the streets today? I ask.

My wife is eating bread. There has been a Flower War, she says without turning around.

From the window of a tall building in the Moorish Quarter, one can see the avenue that leads to the city's centre. The pane is latticed with dark wood, in the style of palaces in Andalus or the Old Maghreb, so that observers can look out but passers-by cannot look in. It is a veil between us and them, between Moor and Mexica, as is so much else in this city of divisions. We crowd around this window now, myself and several dozen other envoys of the caliphate, each trying to jostle forwards for a clearer vision.

In truth I do not exert myself, for I have seen this sight before. This sight, or other sights that have been much the same. The imam is here, gazing down stony-eyed at the scene, and Abd al-Wahid is standing back, hands resting on his belly. I recognise another face as the thin-cheeked fellow from the gate, the one with the shaven upper lip, who took it upon himself to inform me that my wife was home. His name is Hasan, I have learned. I have made enquiries.

There are other younger men, men who have only been in the city for six months or a year, two years, and for whom a Flower War is still a marvellous novelty. They talk in low, excited tones, their arms around each other's backs. Like frightened boys. They look so young.

Malinala is not here, for she is not permitted.

Noises from the street drift up, shouts and celebratory songs. The eager barks of hairless dogs. The slap, slap, slap of feet.

When at last it is my turn to peer down through the grille, I see what I have seen before, which is what I expected. A column of Mexica knights dressed in suits of jaguar skin, moving at a steady jog, bright pennants fluttering at their backs. Each of them pulls a naked captive on a rope.

The captives are jogging too, doing their best to keep the pace, but they appear no less exhausted than the men in front of them. From this distance and this height their features are not visible, but the impression I have, as I have had before, is of an undertaking that is mutually endured. The ordeal seems to be somehow shared. As if the knights and the naked men are bound by more than ropes.

People throw flowers as they pass, and it has never been clear to me who they are intended for. Are they for the conquerors or for their vanquished captives?

That one is bloodied, says a man, pointing at some passing wound.

He will be more so presently, says the man beside him.

A recollection comes to me of the recent caravan, the camels yoked together in lines, loping onwards nose to tail, in the same way as these warriors. One procession flows one way and another flows the next, as if the city were breathing in and breathing out.

I watch for a little while before I am nudged along by someone more impatient than me, a shepherd with reddish hair who came with last year's caravan. I willingly forsake my place but the spectacle does not last. The line of jaguar knights soon passes, absorbed into the city. Some barefoot children run behind, shouting enthusiastically, then the streets fill in again with normal city business.

How many? I ask a man who has been watching all along.

I make it sixty-nine, he says.

Sixty-one, says someone else. Look, I made a note of them, a dash for every man that passed.

Sixty-nine, the first man says. Some of the knights had more than one.

No matter, I say. A small affair. I have seen them in their hundreds before.

In their thousands, says the shepherd.

Do not exaggerate, I say.

Eli, says Abd al-Wahid, approaching me as the crowd thins out. Where might these be taken from?

A naked man is a naked man, I say. They could be from anywhere. But not from Tlaxcala or a place of much significance. Most likely from a peasant town, some Nahua village somewhere.

Like Malinala. From a place of green grass.

There has been a Flower War. There is always a Flower War.

The Flower War is not a war as we would understand a war. The emperor sends out his knights, in their eagle feathers and jaguar skins, but their intention is not to kill but capture. It is a complicated dance, each side manoeuvring skilfully, each warrior setting his sight on a warrior in the opposite ranks and performing graceful steps until he is within reach. The knights' obsidian-bladed clubs, which can cleave a body in one swing, are wielded surgically, to hamstring and to handicap. The greatest glory is to bring a man back whole, undamaged.

I have seen this from afar, when I used to travel more. I have watched from a small hill, shaded by a canopy held by servants of the emperor, surrounded by mushrik noblemen who commented approvingly on successful stratagems, in the way that high-bred Moors might comment on falconry. Moctezuma himself was there, my spyglass pressed against his eye.

Malinala was there as well, eating popped maiz from a bowl.

Her people had been caught like this, food for the gods, for many years, since before she was a girl. It has always been this way. The Nahuas in the lands around pay a tax of blood and slaves to Tenochtitlan. Slaves such as her. Not many are saved as she was. Most give their blood to feed the sun, to keep it spinning in the sky, to keep the world from ending.

Watching my wife sidelong, for a second I thought I saw a shadow on her face, her lip curled, as with distaste.

But then she looked at me and smiled. Would you like popped maiz? she offered.

Chichimecs, someone shouts, coming up the stairs into the room. That is what the gatesman says. They were taken in the north, causing mischief in the hills.

There we are, says Abd al-Wahid, looking pleased with himself. No one of concern to us. Just a tribe of vagabonds.

What Abd al-Wahid means, of course, is no one of concern to trade. We do not deal with Chichimecs as they have nothing that we want, aside, perhaps, from skins and furs that are easily sourced elsewhere. Their culture is not mercantile, unlike that of other mushriks. They do not build in stone, nor build anything at all. They are like untethered beasts, migrating here and there.

Like the Israelites you have described, Moctezuma told me once, half serious and half in jest, during one of our long, perplexed discussions in his palace one night.

If they are Israelites, I replied, then this city is Babylon.

The man with the shaven upper lip, Hasan, is talking volubly. Have you ever seen, he asks, what happens in those temples?

I take a few steps closer, curious what he has to say. A crowd of fools stands about him, eager for his story.

Their bodies are painted green, he says. Their heads are shaved. Then their hearts are cut out of their chests and eaten by the priests. The women and children drink their blood.

They do not drink blood, I say.

Perhaps I should not get involved, but his manner rankles me. Faces turn to look at me.

Neither do they eat their hearts. It is the gods who eat the hearts, when they are burned as offerings. Have you not seen the smoke? It is the gods who drink the blood. Not women and children. Gods.

Other Moors are staring now. I have spoken louder than I meant to.

Well, you should know, says Hasan.

There is silence in the room.

Why should I know? I ask, studying him carefully. Again there is no trace of guile. However, there is something.

You have been here many years, he says. Since the start, they say. You sailed with the founding fleet.

Suddenly I am unsure. His eyes are bright and innocent and his voice is full of praise.

That is true, I say.

So you should know, he says.

The gods, Eli? Another voice. The imam is standing near. He wears a disapproving scowl.

I do not mean it literally, I say. But that is the belief.

Their gods do not exist, he says.

Of course they do not, I say.

Their gods are devils. Djinns, he says.

Indeed they are, I say.

Eli, may I have a word?

It is Abd al-Wahid this time, hovering beside the door. I am glad of the excuse and bid the rest good day. The imam nods testily. I glance at Hasan, who meets my eye and smiles in an easy manner.

Blue, I say as I walk away.

What? he asks.

It is blue, not green. Their bodies are painted blue.

Have you seen the emperor? Abd al-Wahid asks at once.

We are on the floor below in a storeroom filled with bolts of cloth. I have not been in here for years. The windows are boarded up, for what reason I do not know. Heavy dust lies on the floor, criss-crossed by footprints.

I pause before answering. Of course he knows that I have not, for he would have been informed. And of course he knows I know. So why must he ask me this?

I have had no chance, I say. Such meetings take time to arrange.

But have you sent a letter? he asks.

It is in hand, I say.

Hmm, he says, regarding me. In the dim light of the room the whites of his eyes are grey. His face is heavy, his hands plump. Everything about the man is larger than it should be. His nostrils and his eyelashes. Even the pores of his skin, like the dimples in an orange peel. He is like a statue subtly larger than life-sized. He has always been this way, ever since we were young, though his muscles now have run to fat. He is still a powerful man, never mind his years.

It is in hand, he repeats as if testing my words, weighing them on his tongue like a vendor with his scales. If you say so, Eli, then I trust it must be so.

There have been no more reports? I ask.

Not as yet, he says.

He reaches up to fumble at the turban wrapped around his head. His hands untuck one end of it and start to pull the cloth away, unwinding it wrap after wrap, like the freeing of a knot. The cloth unspools at his feet. There must be yards and yards of it. At length his bare pate is revealed, bald but for some wisps of hair, as shiny as mahogany and, again, rather too large. He rubs his skull. Wrinkles spread across it as across a lake.

That is better, he says. I have a tormenting itch. Then he says in a smaller voice, Oh God, this country.

Not knowing what else to say, I say, It is hard, this time of year. The heat.

The heat, he repeats, as if sunk in sudden gloom. He rubs his polished head again, more violently, with both his hands. The heat, he says, the sweat, the smell. The stupid mushriks everywhere. Do you not grow tired of it? Do you not wish we had not come?

I look down at my shoes and wait. I study the patterns in the dust.

Abd al-Wahid gives a groan that is part amusement, part despair. His purple-black eyelids are closed. When his eyes roll up again he appears somewhat restored. And yet, he says, despite it all, I would not return.

Return? I ask.

To Andalus. To some shabby palace by the sea. Not even with my fortune made. Would you?

No, I say.

The caliphate is too small for me, he says. Like a box closed on all sides.

No doubt Benmessaoud feels the same, I say.

Abd al-Wahid stares at me with a startled, sad look on his face. With his hairless head exposed he appears much

75

older. The door is open now, he says, gesturing vaguely with his hands.

So what can we do? I say.

He gazes down at himself, at the sleek weight that he bears, as if regarding something unfamiliar from a height. Then his hands begin to reel his turban-cloth back in. We can but prepare, he says, concentrating on the cloth. The Frowning Lord must be advised as to what this represents, insofar as we can tell. But we do not wish to cause alarm. Alarm is not good for business. So. You should go quietly. Ascertain what he plans to do. And Eli?

Yes? I say.

I am sorry about your wife.

He drapes the cloth about his head so that it hangs down on each side, peering briefly out at me as if he is inside a tent. Then he gathers in the slack, once, twice, thrice about his skull. His nimble fingers tuck and fold, making neat work of it.

It is not me, you understand, he says as he wraps himself back up. A faction of the younger men more lately come from Andalus. They do not trust her as we do. There are rumours going around...

There are always rumours going around, I say.

Of course, of course, he says. There is chatter in the marketplace. The mushriks say a lot of things. Most of it is camel-dung, nonsensical, like their gods. But still, the matter is sensitive. Our position here is delicate. And it is said that the emperor has been acting strange of late.

What would acting normal be, in relation to an emperor? I ask, attempting levity.

Abd al-Wahid gives a lazy glare. Did he seem strange when you last met? he asks.

It was some months ago.

I have heard that he is spending more and more time apart, in that strange black room of his. He sits alone. Brooding, they say. He neglects his court, his governance...

The city functions well, I say.

It must soon do more than function. It must respond, Eli. We depend on you, he says.

His hands perform the final fold. Beturbanned, once again complete, he motions towards the door.

God be with you, he says.

And with you, I say. I trail his robed bulk through the door. When we reach the steep stone steps he goes up and I go down.

Halfway back towards my rooms I recall the ailing girl, but it is too late now. The matter will have to wait.

It is not that Abd al-Wahid's rank is higher than my own. He is the head of the council that governs the Moorish Quarter's trade, and he holds offices such as Chief Vizier, Keeper of the Coin and others that have been invented, and forgotten, over the years, but those titles and positions do not raise him over me. Not officially, anyway. I have titles of my own, such as Chief Interpreter and Ambassador to the Sun, but both of us, in the end, are merely merchants of the caliph, bound by articles of trade, with charters renewed annually.

Between us is equality, or something that is close enough.

Then there is what I am. There is the caliph's law.

The caliph's law is a guarantee of the protections I enjoy as a dhimmi of Andalus, a person of the book. It extends to Christians too, for our God is the same God. The law has held in Andalus since before my father's time, since my father's father's time, when the Frankish armies were at last repelled and the rebels crushed, the northern mountains pacified, and the dominion of the caliph extended to all corners of that yellow and green peninsula that lies between the Middle Sea and the Sea of Darkness. Alchemists, philosophers, physicians and other learned men flocked to thriving Qurtubah from Europe and the Old Maghreb, the Levant, distant India. It was the start of the great peace, the dawn of the Golden Age.

The arc of that prosperity might have passed its zenith now, but we are not yet in night. The caliph's law endures. It stands around me like a wall that both shields and separates.

Like the smiling water-god, I am kept within my bowl.

The bowl, however, is larger here. It soars to the horizon. There are days, weeks, even months when I can hardly see its edge, can almost allow myself to think that its circumference might extend to the wheeling sun, the moon and stars, the precious, secret ores that the earth conceals beneath my feet. The Thirteen Heavens above and the Nine Hells below.

And then there are the other days, when the bowl is cramped again. But those days are fewer here than they were in Andalus.

I would not go back, said Abd al-Wahid.

We are equals in that, at least.

I once held another title too, but I have no use for that one now. As we came across the sea they called me Navigator. I could not read the wind nor stars, nor understand an astrolabe, and I vomited almost constantly. But still the crewmen called me that.

My only claim to their trust was the papers in my hand.

Those papers, now, rest in the iron chest on the shelf in the largest room, where I keep my other precious things. My holy books. My conch-shell. Sometimes it occurs to me that I should burn them one day.

But I could no more turn them to ash than I could the codices.

It is another blazing day, the sunlight ravaging the sky, turning it white and thin. On days like this the lake glowers like a sheet of metal. The call to prayer is sounding as I walk into the street, the muezzin's voice high and clear, undiminished by the heat. Above him, on the heavenward-pointing spear-tip of the minaret, hangs a shining crescent moon that is made of tin.

The flaming sun and the crescent moon, the symbols of Mexica and Moor, of dawn and dusk, of day and night, one raging bright, one cool and still.

One reflecting the borrowed radiance of the other.

Familiar mushriks smile at me as I walk along the street, following the road that was taken by the jaguar knights. They will have reached the temples now, where the solemn priests await. But there will be no smoke today, though Hasan and his foolish friends might watch for it impatiently, for the hour can be determined only by the abstruse calculations of astrologers, horologists and sooth-sayers, and by the emperor himself. It might be weeks or months. Until that time I believe that the captured men will be treated well, for the gods do not want spoiled food.

Their bodies are painted blue, I said. I did not need to say that.

A seller of cactus-fruit goes by, calling to advertise his wares. A wrinkled crone of lowly caste is sweeping away the flowers. Maiz has been scattered too, to greet the knights as they returned, and every time this woman finds a grain she picks it up with care and tucks it inside her gown, which is brown and full of holes. Not far away, a hairless dog is lapping at the dust, to which the taste of blood, or the memory of the taste of blood, has magnetised its fervid tongue. Maiz and blood, the mushriks think, is what the gods shaped men from.

The Flower War can never end, that is what the emperor says, for if it ends the world will end. Blood must be spilled to feed the gods, to keep the sun in motion. Hearts must be harvested or the sun will not come up again.

The system is transactional, like any other trade.

From that latticed window there I have seen them streaming in, the knights with their captured warriors. I could not calculate how many. For twenty years I have watched these things as I have watched the lake, the hills, the bustling of the marketplace, my wife's body as she walks.

The sun has always come up the next day.

The world has not yet ended.

*　　*　　*

She is standing at my desk when I return, her back to me. Her hair, oiled in its knots, has the look of ebony. She has something in her hands. What is this? she asks me.

For a long, peculiar beat I think she has my papers there, and what I feel, as if from far away, is a sense of lightening. But the iron chest's position on the high shelf is unchanged. She turns and holds the object up, and as she does I recall the way in which, the other day, she wrenched a cob of maiz from the floating garden on the lake and wastefully tossed it away. Her eyes have the same light.

Now I see what she has found. It is my abortive letter to the emperor, the two circles that I drew, one black and one white, which is my private code to him.

It represents backgammon.

Are we going to see the Frowning Lord? she asks.

My heart... I say.

This is what I call her during moments of tenderness. She calls me her ugly deer and I call her my heart.

Have you any date in mind? she asks.

I take a breath. Abd al-Wahid, I begin. Or should I say, the council. They have requested that I go to Moctezuma's court, for an audience with the emperor...

Alone, she says.

I hesitate. Yes, alone, I say.

My wife narrows her bright eyes. Her mouth moves in a smile. Very well, she says.

They say the matter is sensitive, I say.

Her smile expands. I expect that he is winning, then? she asks.

I gaze at her, confused.

It must be that he is beating you, and you do not wish your wife to see you lose. At the game, she says.

Ha! Indeed, I say.

She hands the letter back to me. Her eyes have lost their lucency. Here, she says. It seems that you have further work to do on this. I do not wish to take your time. Shall I make some xocolatl?

Thank you, I am fine, I say.

Tea? A cup of cactus wine?

I need nothing, I say.

Then I will run some errands, she says. I shall be gone a little while.

Malinala, I attempt, but she evades my hand and lightly brushes past my arm. Soon she is through the door.

Peace be with you, someone calls as she passes in the yard, but I hear no reply.

That did not go well, I think. But it did not go badly.

Sitting down, I take my pen and grind the ink-stick in its bowl until it makes a pool of ink, into which I dip the nib. I should do this quickly now, for my wife has been duly informed, and she should not complain and certainly should not take offence at this shift in circumstance, which, when all is said and done, is no business of her own. I am her husband, after all. I am Ambassador to the Sun. My name is Eli Ben Abram. My pen inscribes it now.

Underneath the two circles I complete the seven-branched tree which represents the menorah, with the initials E.B.A. above three of its branches. This is the sigil of my house, known from here to Andalus. But the emperor reads no Arabic, though he speaks a few small words, so our missives must be in glyphs, some real and some invented. I draw the symbol for a house, then the symbol for a foot. The house I colour black. My pen waits above the page as I consider the glyph for grass, which is a symbol for my wife, with some negating modifier such as the glyph for air, which might denote a vacancy. But in the end I opt against. It is better to keep things simple.

When the ink is dry I fold the page and melt a blob of sealing wax. It has a reassuring smell, soft in the candle flame. Into the fat crimson drop I press the Moorish Quarter's seal, a crescent moon inside a flaming sun, and fan it dry.

I should feed the water-god. But first, dispatch the letter.

There is no sign of Malinala in the courtyard or the street. I will run some errands, she said. She is always running errands. Hurriedly I make my way south rather than north this time, past the shrine to the Dog-Headed God, which, untypically, is thronged with worshippers today, with mushriks from the villages who must be on a pilgrimage. They have brought fowl to kill. They are burning feathers. The idol gleams with sticky grease, lolling its graven tongue. The god who led the Feathered Snake into the underworld.

My destination is not far. Near the Gate of the South lies the Street of Messengers.

I seek out one I know, a man they call Coyotl. He wears a white band around his head and armlets on his arms, leather sandals bound with thongs criss-crossed almost to the knee.

Take this to the Black House, I say, handing him the letter.

He does not run within my sight, which is a superstition they have. But once he is out of view he will fly with speed and grace, not deviating here nor there, until he arrives at the private court of Moctezuma.

At the shrine as I return the worshippers are chanting now, their words a susurrating drone.

Back outside the Caliph's Gate I glance involuntarily at the latticed window, which is dark. There might be a watcher watching me but one would never know.

A hairless dog is trotting through the gate with something in its mouth. There is no guard again today. Things are getting sloppy. Inside the room nothing has changed, except that the water-god's bowl is no longer on my desk but on the floor, overturned, an island on its own small lake. There is no water-god. Confused, I hurry to the yard to see if there is any sign of an intruder, perhaps a child, and that is when I see again the disappearing hairless dog, which glances back furtively. From between its jaws there hangs a limp, translucent hand.

· FOUR ·

THE steam, ascending from the kettle, dissipates into the air. Its tendrils writhe around the lid like the smoke upon the mountain. The water simmering inside is coming to a rolling boil.

It is not the mountain in my mind but Benmessaoud.

I first heard that name, I think, when we were still in Qubah. News had come across the sea of an uprising back in Andalus, in the Christian provinces of the north. The caliph was not well prepared. His army was defeated. The rebels started marching south, burning mosques and synagogues and committing outrages. Some Muslims living in the south seized their chance to rise as well, commoners and farmers who resented other people's wealth. Gharnatah was besieged. They burned the pomegranate groves. Then they marched on Qurtubah.

Then came Benmessaoud.

Benmessaoud did not come from Andalus but the Old Maghreb, from some flyblown camel-town on the fringe of the endless desert. He was an emir of some kind. They are all emirs down there. I do not know how he amassed an army, let alone a fleet, but both of these things he did. Landing in Andalus, he swore fealty to the caliph.

The next we heard, it was done. The traitors had been defeated. There was talk of executions, severed heads, the usual things. But the peace had been restored. The caliphate was saved.

In Yuqqatan, years afterwards, I met a man who claimed that he had fought alongside Benmessaoud, had seen him on the battlefield. What was he like? I asked.

Smaller than you would think, he said. His manner almost like a clerk. Like someone you would pass on the street and not recall his face. Only his eyes, he said. By his eyes you would know.

Know what? I asked this man.

That he is blessed, he said.

Later still, somewhere else, I met another man who said that he had been on the other side, a Christian soldier from the north. After that I changed, he said, pointing to his hennaed beard, the knitted skullcap on his head. This man had come to the New Maghreb, like other men, to become new.

And what of Benmessaoud? I asked.

He is like fire, he said.

There was no word after that, not for many years. But we were looking west, not east. The sea was like a veil. The further we worked our way into this strange continent, which we knew was not the Indies then, and perhaps had always known, the more the concerns of Andalus shrank into insignificance. Its politics, intrigues and wars. Things that had been large seemed small.

The caliphate grew indistinct, real and yet unreal. Like this pale steam rising up.

The water is almost boiling. Bubbles tap against the lid. Its edges dance and rattle. A hiss begins, high and shrill, with the promise of a scream.

I pour white rice into a pan and check for errant weevils.

Malinala has been absent from my house for three days, since the incident with the bowl. I take my meals alone. I could eat with the other Moors, most of whom have mushrik women to prepare their food for them, and sometimes to share their beds, though this is not publicly spoken of. But I seek no company.

There have been absences before, in the course of our union. She has been gone for weeks. She has even left the city. The first time this occurred I feared that she might be dead, but messengers brought back the news that she had travelled south on some business with the Mayayans. It emerged that she was in negotiation over xocolatl rights, and when she returned to Tenochtitlan it was with a trade agreement. This would have furrowed Moorish brows had the particulars been known. But only Abd al-Wahid knew, and he chose to keep it quiet.

Another time she secured an arrangement with the Zapotecs for the importation of uncut jade, but this displeased the emperor, contravening as it did some customary relationship of which we were unaware. She was called to the Black House. She was ordered there alone. It was an anxious day I waited for her to return, not knowing what the emperor's word might be.

But she returned to me intact. She would not discuss the matter.

With a knife I start to slice tomatl into juicy slabs, laying out its red-black flesh. The knife is of obsidian, knapped to a razor's edge.

The pulpy seeds, wet in the light, remind me of the water-god. That delicate, pellucid meat.

The empty bowl sits on my desk.

The kettle is trembling.

I was living in Mexica the next time I heard his name. Rumours came by caravan, from the mouth of a camel-driver. The fellow had missing teeth, a broken nose, a cretinous stare, and his word was not reliable. These camel-drivers hear all kinds of things upon their wanderings, exchanging news like bags of gold, and much of that gold is false. Yet some of it is true. Benmessaoud had not returned to the Old Maghreb, said this man, but had stayed in Andalus. The Protector of the Caliphate. But he was growing restless. In his eyes the caliph's realm had grown sinful and corrupt, like a beautiful fruit that has rotted on the inside. He denounced the trade in mushrik goods. Xocolatl and tubaq he thought abominations. He spoke ill of the caliph, who he claimed was a drinker of smoke, his purity defiled by the potions of idolators. As long as Benmessaoud remained in Andalus he was a threat. The caliph wanted rid of him, but he could not challenge him.

They say the caliph will send him here, he said. To this New Maghreb.

Later this same camel-driver was heard to declaim that djinns had chased his ship across the sea, and that elephant-sized birds lived on some of the islands there. So his words were not believed.

But some of them stayed with me.

The kettle is fairly shrieking now. A gout of scalding steam bursts out as I lift the lid. I pour the water on the rice and place the pan upon the stove, wipe the black blade of the knife, toss the tomatl slices in. I add chilli from Mexica and salt from Andalus.

Like a box closed on all sides. That is how Abd al-Wahid described our little caliphate. As the water roars again I think about the pent-up heat, the mounting of the steam inside, the pressure crying for release. The trick the caliph has performed. The lifting of the lid.

Lying in the dark, I think. It must have strayed in off the street. Wandered, brazen, through the gate, spied its opportunity.

There was no guard at that time. Why was there not a guard?

An act of God, it might be called. It must have just come strolling in. Snuffling through my open door.

Did I leave it open?

Often I neglect the lock, the lock I bought from Qurtubah, because there is no stealing here. Not like in Andalus. No burglary, at any rate, unless it is by fellow Moors, and that is not unknown. But it is not common.

So often I neglect to lock my door, but I always keep it closed. To stop the lizards from getting in. They get in anyway, of course.

But why was there no guard?

The man who chews the tasty root, the man whose spit is emerald green, I have not seen him for days. He is absent from his duties. Is he drunk on cactus wine? Has he been called away? We live in a time of peace, this is what I tell myself. But we are not asleep.

I am not asleep.

This is the darkest time, an hour or two before the dawn. The darkest and the quietest. The air sags moist and heavy. The blackness infiltrates like oil.

The bed is damp, the sheets awry. My body stings from sweating.

I was woken by a noise. A rustle or a thump. My first thought was Malinala, but it was not Malinala. Perhaps it was not anything. Perhaps it was some rodent.

What was it I was dreaming of to make my body sweat so much? I have not remembered dreams since I came to the New Maghreb. Here, I have no need of them.

In Andalus I dreamed.

It feels as if the world has stopped. No wind, no movement anywhere. As if creation has been stilled, the stars, the ripples on the lake, as if the sun is snagged somewhere and will not return.

For a second I feel a shadow of the fear the mushriks feel, that the sun has lost its appetite, is guttering like an empty lamp and will not renew itself. That its drops of fuel are spent. That this dark will never end. Is this what Malinala thinks?

I am never sure what she thinks, despite the stories that she tells. She tells them well, but after all, they are only stories.

Was it only happenstance that the horrid beast walked in, nose quivering, nudging at the bowl? Did it stand on its hind legs, its forepaws on my desk? I can see the water-god gazing up defencelessly at those pink, descending gums, the long teeth popping its soft skin. Still with that smile on its face. Why was it always smiling?

My wife is angry with me, that is what her absence means. When she is angry she is quiet. So quiet she disappears.

It does not happen often, because I do not give her cause. Not like other husbands with their hard words and their beatings. We have understanding. Trust. I have made her who she is.

She has made me who I am. We have a partnership.

Always she has stood with me when I stand before the emperor. She has sat when I have sat, bowed when I have bowed. From Arabic to Nahuatl, Nahuatl to Arabic. We have had the emperor's ear.

Two links in a chain.

When we crossed the floating road, marvelling at what lay beyond, she was there. Her words were there. She performed the introductions.

When we first met Moctezuma, dazzling in all his gold, Malinala's voice was strong even as mine faltered.

In her first address to the emperor she looked him in the eye, which was a breach of protocol. We had been warned against it. His courtiers were horrified. Abd al-Wahid was horrified. But Moctezuma looked right back, his narrow face expressionless.

When he looked me in the eye, I turned my gaze away.

Two links in a chain, but the chain is broken now. No, not broken. It is nothing that cannot be put back together. But, as Abd al-Wahid said, there is a faction, recently arrived, that does not have faith in her. Those rumours drifting through the streets.

They are only rumours.

She is used to being mistrusted by the Mexica, of course. In their eyes she is still a slave, a Nahua woman caught in war, caught and sold to the Mayayans, and by the Mayayans to us, dishonoured and debased. Now they must witness her gliding through the marketplace, weighing this and checking that, living in the Quarter of the Strangers, with her hair in knots. She has gone from that to this. The Woman of Two Tongues. They observe her on my arm, in the Black House of the emperor. Some call her a sorceress, a trafficker between worlds.

She is used to their mistrust. But not to the mistrust of Moors.

Is she angry or afraid?

How long until the dawn?

I turn one way and then the next. The sheets are hot and clammy. The blackness pushes down on me, seeping into everything, sucking all the light away.

There. It is that noise again. From somewhere in the courtyard.

Has the hairless dog returned, looking for other morsels here? Is it skulking in the dark, sniffing at our doorways? I have never understood why it is the Mexica suffer these creatures close to them. Their plucked, puckered flesh is like dead chicken skin. They are prized and yet reviled, revered as the brothers of men and children of the Dog-Headed God, yet I have also seen them kicked, stoned and spat on.

If they are the brothers of men, why are they whipped and abused? I asked Malinala once.

Are not men also abused? she asked. Are not men also whipped?

Holding my breath, I listen to the darkness beyond the door. The air is still. Not the slightest wind. There is no sound in the courtyard.

Perhaps I imagined it, but still I push aside the sheets and place my bare feet on the floor. My knees crack as I stand, a noise like two small whips. I cross the room and hesitate before the door, not wanting to open it for fear of what might be behind. Then I throw it open.

Nothing scuttles. Nothing flees. There is only blackness.

The door swings back on its hinges, which are in want of oil. They are rusty like my knees. Seventeen years ago that door was hung by Issa's hand, when he was still a carpenter, before he became old like me. When our presence here was young.

When everything was young.

Those were bright, resplendent days. But I cannot think of them tonight. Nor can I think of what might come. All I can do is wait.

My bare feet take me back to bed, where I lie gazing up into the dark, or else gazing down, into the heavens and the hells stacked into infinity, layer after layer of them. Hours or minutes pass. I do not think of hairless dogs or

Benmessaoud or the stricken girl or the smoking mountain or my wife. I do not sleep. Perhaps I sleep. At last, the faintest glow.

It comes inching through the cracks, grain by grain, gaining ground. One could not yet call it light. It is the dream of light. It seeps, spreads, consolidates, the blackness bleeding into blue.

At last, so sweet my heart could burst, there comes the call to prayer.

The glyph denoting Tenochtitlan is a cactus on a rock, which alludes to the founding story of the city. The glyph consists of three fleshy lobes projecting crimson thorns, each crowned with its golden flower. Next to it is a house with two red dots beside it. This signifies that Tenochtitlan was founded in the year 2 House, which corresponds to 725 in the Islamic calendar, or to 1325 in the reckoning of Christians. The rabbi, bless his memory, would have called it 5085. With the stone solidity of its streets, its temples hard against the sky, it is easy to forget that this city is not two centuries old, younger than any city I ever knew in Andalus. Its builders have not been here long. Like us, they are strangers.

The codex I am working on relates to the early struggles they had, following their long migration southwards from their homeland. The glyphs of footprints, black upon the earth, ended at this lake, whose glyph is a double flower, but the lake was not unoccupied. There were older cities here, established in their power. The enemies of the Mexica first gave them land in a place that was infested with snakes, hoping the snakes would poison them, but the Mexica killed the snakes and cooked them on their spear-tips. That is what the glyphs relate. Then the others feared them.

The years went by. 1 Knife. 12 Rabbit. The other cities fell. This codex, scribed on deerskin, documents the wars, retreats, conquests and alliances that saw the People of the Sun spreading from this marshy isle, where the eagle killed the snake, to fill the valley of the lake beneath the smoking mountain. It tells a history not unlike, as Moctezuma has observed, the fall of the walls of Jericho, the destruction of the Canaanites, the coming of God's people to the country that was promised them. The land of milk and honey. Of gold and xocolatl. The temple of your Solomon, he once asked as we sat together, is it like the temples that you see here, by our Rack of Skulls?

I do not know, I replied, for I never laid eyes on it. It was destroyed long ago.

And so you have come here to ours, he said, laying down his piece.

The conversations we have had, over our backgammon games! They have ranged unboundedly, into unexpected places. Though he was once a warrior, as is the precondition here, the emperor called the Frowning Lord is a wise and cultured man, educated in philosophy, poetry, theology, the sacred arts of writing, mathematics and astronomy. Of course, he is a god as well.

But there are many gods.

I once suggested jokingly that Tenochtitlan was Babylon, but perhaps, as I read these codices, it is more

Jerusalem. Not Jerusalem as it was but Jerusalem as it might have been, reflected in the obsidian orb that the mushriks call a smoking mirror, a black inversion of our own. Perhaps it is even Makkah. I would never suggest such blasphemies to my countrymen, but it is the kind of thing that the emperor mulls upon. Time is not straight but cyclical, according to the Mexica, and the world, as has been known to Moorish scholars for many years, is not flat but spherical, which is a type of endlessness. If one keeps going west one ends up in the east.

Black footprints scrawled across the earth.

From nothing came two things.

I am staring at the glyphs, but they have lost their meanings now. The edges of them bend and swell. Their inked lines overflow. I am hunched over my desk, thinking of too many things. I did not sleep well last night.

I put down my pen.

It is well past sunrise now, and the Moorish Quarter hums with the usual traffic of the day, the slap of leather soles on stone. I shut the codices. Malinala has been absent for four nights, or is it three? The bowl of the water-god is empty, a reminder.

After breakfasting on dates I take the pestle in my hand and grind the customary beans. I toss them lightly in the pan. The aroma is not the same. Malinala does it better, as she does most everything, and as I grind I repeat the words of our small ceremony.

How long?

Too long.

How long now?

Long enough.

Long enough. I take a sip. The familiar darkness rises. The xocolatl is adequate but it is nothing more than that, there is no ritual to be shared, no head to rest upon my arm as the vigour climbs my veins. Sometimes when I take my cup I feel as the emperor must feel, a god, ascending among gods, but I do not feel this way today. I only feel alone and old, bent in an empty room.

Peace be with you, someone says.

I open my eyes. A boy stands there. Do you require more worms? he asks in Nahuatl.

What is it about this boy? Something that unsettles me. No more worms, I say.

He stares at me defiantly, in the way that children do. No worms, I say again. Run along now. Go.

Reluctantly he turns away, dragging his long toes in the dust, and that is when I see, again, his back. The marks upon it. They have grown more angry now and spread across his arms, his neck. His skin has a sallow sheen. His hair is like a mop.

But is it the same boy? I am suddenly uncertain. Not all mushriks look the same, despite what some Moors like to say, but their children look the same, or at least they look alike, or at least they do to me, who never has had to deal with them.

Here, I say.

In hope he turns.

Would you like some dates? I ask.

He shambles quickly through the door as if I might soon change my mind, and as I take some shrivelled fruits and place them in his greedy hands I recognise that he is not the boy who came before. They are like small guilds, these children, hoarding opportunities. He might eat half of these dates and give the rest to others. He is not the same boy but the blotches on his back, his arms, his neck, they are the same. Or at least they are alike.

Do your friends have marks like these? I ask quietly.

His eyes widen in alarm and he twists away from me, the dates clutched tightly in his fist.

Wait! I say, but he is through the door, out across the courtyard and through the Caliph's Gate, which has a guard again today. He is not the usual man but he is in position nonetheless, the scimitar in his hand, more a symbol than a sword. He makes no objection to the child's passing.

Is everything well, Eli? asks my neighbour from Ishbiliyya, the silk merchant, squinting from his step.

Everything is well, I say, ducking back into my quarters.

On the floor lies a date that the boy dropped in his haste, and as I stoop to pick it up I think of the maiz-cake that I dropped outside the house of the stricken girl a week ago, or was it more? One morsel scattered here, one there. It seems to me that there has occurred some mysterious exchange.

No message has arrived for me? I ask the guard as I walk by.

Who are you? he asks.

The question amazes me. I am Eli Ben Abram, I say.

He stirs and gives a grunt.

This guard is an ox-like man, thick-browed, with stupid eyes. A dagger hangs at his waist, not curved but straight, in the Frankish style. I have heard of you, he says. You came with the founding fleet.

I led the founding fleet, is what I want to say. But instead I say, I am waiting for a message.

The sturdy man regards me but does not exactly meet my eye.

From the Black House, I say.

His face remains unmoved.

From the court of the emperor, I say, impatience in my voice.

Nothing has come, he says.

God willing it will soon, I say. Inform me when it does.

He nods ponderously, once. Frustrated, I push past him. There is no sign of the boy, and there is little to be gained from going in pursuit of him. But still I need to walk to give myself some purpose. I am not in the frame of mind to venture to the marshy place that is my place of solitude, which is now rife with flies. Nor to the place of willow trees. But I must go somewhere. Some days ago a confidant informed me that the uli-sellers have arrived from the south, as they do every year, to sell their wares by the court of games. And so I wander that way now. The walk is not too far. The street is full of commoners barging this way and that, officials of the emperor with their feather-headed staffs, but I only see the crowd as a cloud of teeth and eyes, teeth and hair, drifting past, sometimes parting to allow me passage and sometimes closing up. Some turn to me, some do not. I have grown indifferent.

Dhimmi! someone cries, but it is a mushrik voice and he does not know what it means, has only learned the syllables. I raise my hand but do not turn. There is delighted laughter.

Moors do not often come to this place, the court of games. The imam disapproves of it, and certain mushriks, in the past, have been hostile to our presence. But there is no game today. The court is bare and empty. Across the waste of level ground stand high walls on either side, each with its hoop of stone carved with the forms of grinning snakes reaching around to bite their tails, like the ouroboros symbol that is known to alchemists. Other than these details there is no embellishment.

The uli-sellers have strung their awnings between the court and the marketplace. They sit quietly in the shade, some women and some men. They are serious and grave, dressed in green travelling cloaks, long-faced, chewing their maiz.

Has your road been fair? I ask.

It has brought us here, they say.

I do not address them in Nahuatl but in Mayayan. They must have walked the land for many weeks to be here. The soft-hard uli that they sell is the product of a tree that grows a long way to the south, which is milked for its precious sap. It is called the tree that weeps.

We first encountered this strange stuff when we were in Yuqqatan. The groves of trees were owned, and milked, by the masters of Malinala. The ones who sit before me now are not the same as I knew then, not the ones from whom I bought my wife with Moorish merchandise. They

speak a different dialect. They are a different nation. Once
mighty like the Mexica, with their own great empire, they
are a scattered people now. Peasants. But still noble.

Gravely the Mayayans watch as I take an uli-ball
and depress it with my thumb. Its black flesh shrinks,
rebounds.

May I sample it? I ask.

If it pleases you, they say.

I fling it sharply at the ground. The sphere meets the
hardened earth and leaps back to the same height, then
falls again, then leaps back, then falls again, then leaps
back. Each time it ascends again it reaches only half the
height. At last it trembles on the ground, its velocity
dissipated.

A wonderful thing, I say.

They blink their solemn eyelids.

This uli substance is unlike anything we have seen
before. It has a tensile quality as if it holds energy. The
harder it is flung away the more abruptly it jumps back. It
is chiefly utilised by players of the sacred game, in which
young men, lithe and beplumed, endeavour to propel
these balls through the snake-embellished hoops that pro-
trude from either wall, not by means of throwing them
but by exertions of their hips, their thighs and other body
parts. It is a spectacle. As with the Flower War, which is
not really a war, this sport is not really a sport but a dance
of symbols. The ball represents the sun, and the purpose
of the players is not to obstruct its flight but to assist its
passage on a predetermined course, a trajectory fixed by
the gods. To interfere with this design is a blasphemy. The

losing players must give their heads. The winning players must take them. At least that is what is claimed. I have never seen it happen. I have only seen young men tumbling in the dust, jerking their strong limbs about, while spectators whoop and jeer.

Perhaps, to mushriks, Moorish pastimes might look just as foolish.

In previous years I have purchased quantities of these strange balls and sent them back to Andalus to be sold as curiosities. I sent one to the caliph once and was told that it amused him. But that is not the purpose of my coming here today.

What news from your country, friends? I ask out of courtesy.

Our country is green, they say, which is what they always say.

Is it a time of peace or war?

It is peace.

The gods be thanked. There is no word of strange events? I ask.

They blink and stare.

The Mayayan women have tattoos on their lips and chins, the men blue dots beneath their eyes. It is the men who answer me but it is the women who watch.

It is said that other Moors have come across the sea, I say. Men like us but not like us. They have sailed along your coast, where the old temples stand. Have you seen them? Have you heard?

The men do not say anything.

The women only watch.

Putting down the uli-ball, I take another from the stall. This one is larger, heavier, and takes both hands to lift.

I hold the uli in my hands, that weight that wants to fall to earth. These Mayayans do not have news. I will learn nothing from them. Speaking in their formal tongue, which I use rarely now, and differs more from Nahuatl than Hebrew does from Arabic, is something from another life. It is years since I learned it. It is the language in which I spoke my first words to my wife, before she was my wife, as she brought the tubaq pipe at the instruction of the lords she served, who were our hosts and allies then.

The pipe was passed around the room. Our council was concluded. As I drew the bitter smoke into my lungs, and heaved it back, as the world plunged nauseously and swum with my tears, this girl's face held in my mind. It struck me like clear water. It seemed the only point of stillness in the whole revolving room, and, although the giddiness did not last long, and sense returned, her presence seemed an anchor and a reassurance somehow.

Water, I said, when I could speak again.

The Mayayan lords were laughing at me, and my countrymen laughed too, even though many of them had coughed as I had done. Malinala also wore a smile as she filled my cup. But it felt as if her smile were for me and not for them.

Water was the first word that I ever spoke to her. I do not remember what the second was, the third, the fourth. The next words I remember were in the place of weeping trees.

It must have been two or three weeks later, or a month at most. Our expedition was preparing to move west again. Trade arrangements had been made with the kingdoms of the Mayayans, Qubah and the Qarib islands seemed a distant memory, and other markets drew us on. It was a kind of fever. The New Maghreb grew vaster on our unformed maps, and in our minds, with every step that we took, every story that we heard. Its horizons were unending. I had walked with Malinala to a grove of uli trees that lay above the smoke-wreathed town. I had asked to see this place, and her masters bade her take me.

Did her masters know, perhaps? Had they seen me glancing at her? It seemed that every time I turned my head I saw her standing there, even when I closed my eyes. Especially when I closed my eyes.

Here is the place, she said.

The trees stood all around us, rising through the morning mist. Their trunks were slim and straight. The grove was deserted. Into each tree's outer flesh a spiralling groove had been cut, out of which the milk-white sap flowed down into a bowl. Most of the grooves were dry and the bowls had been gathered in, but one had been left behind. The sap still dribbled from the trunk. The bowl had overspilled.

Malinala watched me as I reached out to touch the sap, which had a springy quality, partly dried and partly wet.

We eat of the earth, she said. Then the earth eats us.

What is it that you mean? I asked.

It is a saying of my people.

I wiped my finger on my robe. The leaves above were very green. The mist flowed damp and cool. She reached for me, or I for her, I do not remember which. Her hands were rough to the touch because they were working hands. With her black hair close to me, not braided then but loose and long, I noticed strands of grass in it and wondered why she had them there. The ground was soft. Winged insects danced and shimmered over us.

I do not come from here, is what she told me afterwards.

We are like each other then, I said.

No, she said.

No. I remember that. She spoke it very strongly. I did not know what to make of it, the forcefulness behind that word, but as she took my hand again, and drew it to herself again, it did not matter much.

The sun probed through the mist.

I drop the heavy uli-ball lightly back onto the stall, where it judders to a stop. Strange, that the sap is white but the finished sphere is black. The Mayayans are looking at me blankly, unexpressively, gnawing at their yellow cobs, turning them over in their hands.

Take me with you, Malinala said.

I took her with me.

We have not seen. We have not heard, says one of the Mayayans, the man who appears to be the one with most authority. I have forgotten what he means. Then I remember. News. No news.

Until the next sun, I say and begin to turn away, when the air thickens with a distant rumbling. It sounds like a wheeled cart rolling down a cobbled hill, but there are no carts in this city, for the Mexica do not use wheels, and neither are there hills. The uli-sellers rise to their feet and stare uncertainly.

There, one of the women says.

A far-off fist of smoke.

It does not appear to move but stands solid in the sky. It grows without seeming to grow, expands without expanding. The Mayayans are talking with each other softly, urgently, not using words I know but another dialect, a tongue to be used secretly. They do not look at me again. I might as well have vanished. I cross the empty court of games between the waiting hoops, with my eyes upon the sky.

The city carries on.

The smoking mountain has not vented flame for twenty years. It sleeps and wakes, the mushriks say. For years it has been sleeping. When we first came to Tenochtitlan it was awake, belching clouds, ashy intermittent bursts that sometimes drifted on the breeze to dull the surface of the lake. We tasted powder on our tongues. Sometimes the sky glowed red like a secondary sunset. Some among my countrymen offered up prayers to God, while the priests of the Mexica increased their efforts at the temples, which, being pyramids, reflect the mountain in their forms, and, on auspicious days, emit smoke like the mountain too. Perhaps the prayers did their work. Or perhaps the temple priests did. The latter is blasphemous to say, but the mountain ceased its noise and no longer troubled us, falling back into its sleep.

Now, if the signs are true, it is waking up again.

But it lies far across the lake, too far away to bother us, that is what I tell myself as I walk back to my quarters. Were its flames to overspill they would extinguish in the lake, like molten metal plunging into water in a forge. But if smothering clouds of dust were to drift across the countryside, to block the light of the sun...

There are closer things to worry about. My absent wife, for one thing.

The Mexica in the streets are muttering, glancing at the sky, where the cloud-smoke stands immobile like a distant statue. Watching it I am reminded of those storms in the Qarib Sea, where the wind known as the huracan rages once or twice a year, ripping up the flailing palms and turning the sky black with clouds that bloat and boil above the sea, billowing up like corals. It is a fearsome thing to see. Twice it destroyed our harbour there, and some seven years ago it wrecked a departing merchant fleet somewhere off the Quban coast, in which myself and others had invested heavily. We received the news by messenger.

When will the message come?

He is still there, the bull-necked guard with the Frankish dagger at his side, and I do not greet him as I pass beneath the archway. But I have not gone several steps before he calls me back.

There is someone waiting here for you, he says.

I turn. He inclines his head towards a figure by the gate, a woman rising from the shade.

I do not know what she wants, he says. I cannot understand her.

The figure reaches out for me. Her arms are bent and skinny. With embarrassment I see it is the lowly woman from the house in the neighbourhood of ducks, the mother of the stricken girl, and before I can prepare myself she is almost through the gate, her fingers clutching at my clothes, lurching forwards into me as I stumble back. Please, she wails, please, my lord, have you asked Him? Does He know? What does the God of Strangers say?

Woman, get back, I say, alarmed by her indignity. There is panic in her eyes. Her spittle flies like mist. I do not want her hands on me, and I try to push them away, but she reaches out for me. He will help, my God will help, I say, but then she jerks away and her body hits the ground with a hollow thump. The guard is standing over her.

She is possessed, he says.

The scimitar jumps in his hand and for a second, in my mind, I can see him bring it down in a single shining arc and cut her clean in two, can see her red guts pouring out. But he does not do that. The woman is crawling in the dust, whimpering pathetically, and I try to go to her, but the guard's thick forearm keeps me back.

She means no harm, I say.

She will do none, he says.

Go home, I call in Nahuatl, though she does not seem to hear. Go and comfort your sick child. I can only do what I can.

Then I turn and walk away without looking back.

The incident has caused a stir on both sides of the gate, like a rock dropped in a pond, but the ripples do not reach far. In steps I have outwalked them.

The familiar courtyard comforts me with its cracked tiles and its lemon trees, its dripping bedding strung from lines. By the useless fountain sit some merchants smoking tubaq. Water bubbles in the bowl. Two of the men are arguing and the others listening. A Berber muleteer goes by, heading for the stables where the baggage animals are kept, the deer, ugly, swift and strong, that did not leave with the caravan. I pass the entrance to the mosque.

The hair beneath the carpet.

The memory brings me to a halt and I am about to duck inside to retrieve the horrid thing before someone finds it there, but there are shoes set on the step. I glimpse pale soles within. Disposing of the hair must wait. I think of the woman in the dust. Her sweat.

The pustules on her face.

I can only do what I can.

The door to my quarters is ajar. The first thought that comes to me is that the hairless dog is back, but hairless dogs do not bring flowers. There are lilies on the table. Fat white lilies from the lake, pale like the soles of the upturned feet inside the mosque.

She turns to me in her white dress.

My man of dust, she says.

The First Sun died when the Feathered Snake pulled the Smoking Mirror from the sky, ashamed by his one-leggedness. There was no more sun. Everything was at an end, she says.

It is almost night. The scent of lilies fills the room. I am lying on the bed while my wife sits next to me.

Everything was at an end, she says. Everything was new.

The lilies are glowing in the dusk in their bowl upon my desk. Insects rasp beyond the walls like multitudes of saws. From the stagnant fountain come the rattling burps of lusting frogs clutching at each other's slimy bodies in the dark. Outside the Moorish Quarter the city is sliding into sleep.

Malinala has come home. Everything is new.

Now it was the turn of the Feathered Snake to be the sun, she says. His body burst into flames. He burned as bright as day. The Second Sun was not weak, was not crippled. He was strong. Men began to walk the earth, to eat, to pray, to copulate. They gave their blood to the gods. And the nights followed the days.

She is not telling this in Nahuatl but in Arabic. You do not want my tongue, is what she said earlier. You do not want my tongue, so I will speak in yours.

It is not me, I tried to say. The council...

The Old Men of the Nose, she interrupted scornfully.

I would have your tongue, I said. I would have every part of you.

Then I will tell a story, she said as she gathered up the flowers, neatly snapping off their stems, spreading their petals in the bowl. I will tell a story and we will speak no more of this. It is a short one for tonight. You look tired. I am tired.

I am tired, yes, I said.

She placed the lilies in the bowl, the bowl that housed the water-god. No mention of its emptiness. She did not look at me.

But the years went by, she says, and men forgot about the gods. They forgot their offerings. They forgot to give their blood. So the Smoking Mirror punished them by turning them into beasts, into monkeys without speech. The Feathered Snake looked down and was angered by what he saw. In his rage he drew a breath and summoned up a mighty wind.

Like a huracan, I think. But I do not interrupt.

He blew the monkeys from the earth, leaving it scorched and bare, she says. Lifeless. So that nothing grew. Then his fire died. That was the end of the Second Sun, when the world was filled with emptiness.

Where have you been? I want to ask.

But like a monkey without speech, I do not say anything.

· FIVE ·

A MAN dressed in another man's skin is walking down the road, rattling a yellow gourd filled with hard percussive beans. He takes three steps and shakes the gourd, takes three steps and shakes the gourd. It makes a harsh, clashing sound like gravel flung against a wall. A woman goes ahead of him, guiding him, for his eyes are closed as if he were walking in his sleep, as if this were some awful dream. His mouth, however, is gaping wide.

A greasy rain is falling.

It drizzles horizontally, washing in across the lake, clammy and unseasonable. The still canal is stippled. On the far side of the lake the shoreline has been smudged away, its tribute-paying villages removed, as if they had been cleansed. The smoking mountain, and its smoke, are gone, as if they never were.

As if nothing ever was.

The street is shining, empty.

In the shelter of a wall I have stopped to watch it pass, this procession that consists of two people and three skins.

The gourd-shaker wears a wooden hat of intricate design, layered with spiked galleries. His face is painted red and grey. His earlobes are shredded. The human garment that he wears is tailored snug around his form, so that his arms are inside its arms, his chest inside its chest, and only at the lower arms do the epidermises diverge, where its empty hands flap loosely off his wrists. Like his closed eyes and his open mouth, it is a metaphor. The wetness gleams upon his skin, and on the skin that is not his. The woman goes ahead of him. Her lips move. I think she might be singing.

They pass across the little bridge without knowing I have seen them.

As I step from my hiding place something moves across the street, in the darkened doorway of a room. A mushrik man is watching there, an artisan of some kind. He stares at me, and I at him, separated by the rain but joined by the act of seeing this, the man with two sets of skin shuffling blindly in his awkward three-stepped dance, rattling his gourd, with the singing woman leading him. It is as if a secret has been shared. I raise my hand in greeting. But the watching face retreats, sliding slowly back into the dimness of the room as if it has evaporated, leaving me with just the rain.

I sense his eyes upon me as I walk the other way.

It is three days since the rain began. The temples drip. The mosque's dome gleams. The mushriks speak in whispers. The seeping clouds have brought a quietness to Tenochtitlan, ordinarily so bright and loud, and the smoke of cooking fires hangs baggy, weighted by the rain.

The island city is becalmed, as if it were a ship at sea. Caught inside a bank of cloud, we cannot see what lies beyond. All we can do is wait.

It is three days since the mother of the stricken girl accosted me and was accosted in her turn. I have not seen her since. The messenger, Coyotl, has brought me nothing from the emperor, a delay that puzzles me. It is three days since my wife returned.

Our house has been at peace.

We have sat by candlelight, conversing about this and that. The progress of the caravan. Contained, domestic matters. She has lifted morning cups of xocolatl to my lips, its flavours balanced perfectly, and smiled at me through the steam ascending from its surface. She has scrubbed and squeezed my feet. I have stroked her hair. She has mentioned nothing of my missive to the emperor, and I have not questioned her on the sad fate of the water-god. Inside these silences is peace.

All peace is built on silence.

I find myself thinking of the Christian bells of Andalus, stifled by the caliph's law, of the wars their stifling must have spared in the history of the caliphate. I think of our muteness at what happens in those temples. The things from which we turn away, not watching and not listening. A balance, Abd al-Wahid says. Within our silence we are safe.

How long will we stay silent?

The rain runs slickly down the walls. Fat droplets smack the tiles. The lilies are browning at their tips, their sweet scent cloying in the room, their freshness mingled with decay. We sit and watch the stripes of water streaking past the doorway.

I saw the Flayed One, I say.

Malinala frowns at me.

Not the god, I say. The man. The man who dresses as the god. He was walking down by the canal.

His eyes were closed? she says.

I nod. There is a battered moth circling around the door, clumsily scraping the walls. It flutters out into the rain then turns and staggers in again.

His mouth was open, she says.

I nod again.

There is a sickness in the district of the jade-mongers, Malinala says, motioning the moth away.

I do not know how she knows these things, but she always knows these things.

The Flayed One will be going there to eat up the disease, she says. They are rich enough to pay his fee.

What kind of sickness? I ask.

That is why his eyes are closed. So he does not see, she says.

In the stories it is told that the skinless god shed his skin so that men could eat what was inside, like a maiz husk being peeled. Inside, his flesh was golden. There is a temple to him here, at the foot of the Temple of the Sun, but it is rare to see his priests active in the light of day. Their services are specialised.

Whose skin is that? I ask. Why are you laughing?

Malinala's smile fades as suddenly as it came, a brief flash passing over. Her hand swipes at the moth again but the creature flaps away.

You ask such foolish things, she says. It is no one's skin.

We are both thoughtful for a while. The water dribbles on and on.

And then she says in the same voice, It is all our skins.

And now I think this is the time to tell her of what I have seen, the children with their blooming sores, the woman with pustules on her face, the girl in the neighbourhood of ducks for whom I promised I would pray, about whom I could find no words. Whose mother was thrown into the dust. Who might be dead by now. I should tell my wife these things, as I should tell her everything. But something stops my tongue. The silence holds me still.

She knows, of course. She must know, for her eyes are everywhere. How could she not? Like all of us, she has seen these things before. In the country of the Mayayans, and further, trailing like a wake through the lands the Moors have crossed, through Qubah and the islands of the Qarib Sea where we first sailed, the sickness followed everywhere.

Everywhere but here.

When we arrived in Mexico I kept watch for it anxiously, praying I would see no signs. Our little quarter grew. The years went by. I saw no signs. The caravans went back and forth, conveying Moorish luxuries, but the sickness did not come. In time I forgot to pray. Perhaps the Mexica, I thought, possessed some vigorous quality that lent them greater fortitude than the other mushriks of these lands, a belief they strongly held themselves. Or perhaps the mountains were a shield, or the xocolatl more sustaining. I even entertained the thought that God had given His blessing to our amity in Tenochtitlan, that the lack of sickness was His sign.

Now, it seems, it has arrived.

Can the Flayed One swallow it? With his open mouth, his coat of office made from some vanquished warrior brought to Tenochtitlan and peeled, dehusked like a maiz cob, the inside matter tossed away and the outer layer preserved. Whose skin is that? I asked. Of course the question was absurd. Malinala laughed at me.

I should tell her what I know.

As if in imitation of the lord of blisters and disease, or at least the man performing him, I open my mouth to speak, but Malinala gives a yelp and beats her hands upon her hair. The fat moth tumbles out of it. It scrapes and circles on the floor. I should tell her everything, but instead I hold my words and watch as she picks it up, fizzing, by a single wing, and throws it through the open door. It lands in a shallow pool with raindrops falling around it.

Those jade-mongers are Zapotecs, says Mohammed Issa through the steam.

Indeed, I say.

They are not from here. Perhaps they brought it with them.

No, I say. It is the same as we have witnessed in Qubah, in the Taiyno villages there. The red lumps, the sores, the smell...

There are many reasons for a smell, says the man who sits across from me.

There are many reasons for lumps and sores, says Issa. It might be flies, perhaps? The flies are pestilent this year.

It is not flies, I say.

Between these tiled walls, half a dozen naked men, sweat-varnished, wallow in the light. Wet steam clouds the chamber. The bodies of my countrymen have an unreal quality, gloaming shapes that do not look like men, their edges blurred. Beards drip. Flesh colours merge.

The rain still falls outside.

In Yuqqatan I saw a man with wasps' eggs laid inside his skin, says Issa. They grew inside his arm. One day they hatched and flew away. It was a marvellous sight. He died, he adds after a pause. But that was not the reason.

Might the sickness not result from jade? interjects another man, a portly Riffish carpet-seller known for his strange ideas. Miners of certain ores suffer from deadly ailments. It is well attested to with lead. Jade has a sickly quality...

It is neither wasps nor jade, I say. It is what we have seen before.

The carpet-seller heaves a sigh. We do not know, he says.

The bathhouse is situated just outside the city wall, near the lake, from which a wooden pipe brings in fresh water. It is a poor replica of the bathhouses of Andalus with their white marble slabs and intricately patterned tiles, their pools of different temperatures, their fragrant and indulgent oils, but at least it keeps us clean. As such, it serves its purpose. My countrymen purify their bodies here before their prayers, and in the past some have voiced objections to my presence. The younger men. Not all of them. But I ignore these mutterings. I need the steam as much as them for my aches and pains.

The Mexica were sympathetic when we asked to build this place. We discovered that they build bathhouses of their own. In rounded rooms made out of mud they sit and swelter as we do, praying to the Goddess of Bright Sweat and other deities, or so I have been told. I have never been inside one. Their religion sets great store in sweat, as it does in blood, as a godly offering. They highly value cleanliness.

In this we are aligned.

One of the younger merchants rises, covering his loins, and tosses water on the glowing brazier from a wooden pan. Steam leaps into the air. I see the smoking mountain. A wave of wet heat escalates, rolling to the corners of the room and rolling back again, and my nostrils and my earlobes burn with a sizzling pain. My skin prickles at the pores. I feel the sweat-drops bulging out.

Aah, Mohammed Issa sighs.

Everything melts away.

When the intensity has passed my head is resting in my hands, and my hands upon my knees. My body is slumped forward. Eli? comes Issa's voice, and I raise my eyes to see him peering at me from inside a vaporous cloud, glistening, with wet white wool upon his chest. I cannot think where I am. The dizziness falls and rises.

Well, dhimmi? asks the man brandishing the wooden pan, and I have a memory of two things simultaneously, unconnected incidents separated by twenty years, thirty years, from chapters of my life that were over long ago. I am hanging from the prow of the first ship, gazing down at silver fish in the shallows of the Qarib Sea, wiping vomit from my chin. I am seeing Malinala's face through a wreath of tubaq. As those past impressions fade, a third remembrance comes to me, of the day when Abd al-Wahid and myself, as honoured guests, first saw the bodies tumbling down the blood-washed temple steps, limb over limb, their faces blue, with red holes where their hearts had been.

Moctezuma turned to me, proffering a plate of fruit. You do not grow bored of this? he asked in his tongue.

You do not grow bored of this? Malinala asked in mine.

Eli, are you unwell? says Issa. Are you sick?

God willing I am fine, I say.

Reeling from the heat, I gaze around at the sweating torsos of my countrymen, in their differing tones of flesh. I take a drink of water. In another point in time I can see these bodies skinned, worn by sightless, shuffling priests rattling their yellow gourds. It is all our skins, is what Malinala said. If the sickness spreads, I think, there will be more offerings, more blood and hearts to feed the sun. They will fight the Flower War. And Benmessaoud is coming.

God willing, comes the voice of the young man with the pan, his eyes gleaming bright. We all know whom the sickness takes. It is in the hands of God, and God is merciful. He strikes down whom He strikes down. It is righteous that He does. But the faithful shall be spared.

My sweat runs like hot rain.

* * *

Outside in the wet I watch the steam curling off my naked arms, my chest, my hands. My body calms and cools. The floating gardens, with their dripping rows of maiz, are square and grey, neatly quartered out across the lake like tethered fleets of ships. The surface of the water swells with overlapping circles.

A mushrik woman hurries past with a green leaf over her head, vainly attempting to stay dry.

On the lake a fisherman casts a net from his kanoa.

Who is that fellow who talked of God? I ask Issa as he cools next to me.

Issa rinses off his sweat from the cistern of lake water.

Not one of those I know, he says. From last year's caravan, I think. I do not know his trade.

He rubs his head with a towel, which is pointless in the rain. He is friendly with Hasan, he says.

Indeed, I say.

The other merchants have returned indoors and it is just us two, old friends standing in the rain. The bath-house coals have lost their heat. My body glows, purified.

This Hasan, I say as I am pulling on my clothes, the material of which feels rough and grimy on my skin, which is tender from the heat. What do you know about him?

He is young and confident, says Issa. At least, he talks a lot.

He listens a lot too, I say. Maybe he is one to watch.

Why do you say that?

I do not know, I say.

Issa stares at me as if expecting something more, but I can give him nothing more.

Perhaps I am just old, I say. And he is young.

That is enough, Issa says with one of his rasping laughs. Perhaps it is just jealousy.

Perhaps it is, I say.

Our bodies damp beneath our clothes, we go together up the road.

Eli, Issa says as we pass the place of willow trees. About the thing you talked about. I did not mean to doubt it. They say three people died this week, in the quarter of the silversmiths. And one last night, a warrior. An eagle knight of some renown. But I did not want to speak of it, or not yet, anyway. Abd al-Wahid has cautioned us not to cause alarm.

If it is happening, I say, it will change everything.

Not all change is bad, he says.

This is bad, I say.

For them, he says. It does not touch us. You know that. Only them. We are somehow steeled for it.

There is no them and us in this, I say. The crescent moon inside the sun. Our fortunes are the same...

They are not the same, he says.

I am surprised by his words, this old and kindly friend of mine. I say nothing for a while. He walks along beside me. But presently he says, My wife died from it, you know. Long ago in Qubah. My child too. It was after we had left. I did not learn the news for years.

I did not know that, I say.

It is in the past, he says.

We approach the city gate, the Gate of the Left-Handed Hummingbird. The street has partly flooded and we have to skirt the edges. A pair of wet-flanked hairless dogs shiver in an alcove there, making both of us recoil, but the creatures do not snarl or growl. They have a hopeless, wretched look. I almost feel sorry for them.

Then I recall the water-god and I do not feel sorry.

Are you afraid? Issa asks after we have walked some more. For clever Malinala's sake?

His words surprise me again. I say nothing but think, Yes. Yes, I am afraid.

But not for Malinala.

Overnight the rain has stopped. The day dawns pale and clear. A distant streak of greyish cloud is visible far to the north, smearing the atmosphere below, raining on the Chichimecs, perhaps, in their deerskin tents. But the valley and the lake have emerged on the other side. Everything is sharp and clean. The hills and mountains are precise, as if their outlines have been inked by an adept calligrapher.

Washed stonework steams in the hot sun.

The smoking mountain smokes.

Look, the weeping warrior, a woman says to her child as I approach the marketplace. Both of them are looking east. Their eyes are on the smoke.

The story that the mushriks tell is of a brave young warrior who went away to fight a war. He was gone for many years and his lover thought him dead. She died of grief, and when at last he returned he died as well, and the gods turned them both to stone and scattered them with snow. The warrior became the smoking mountain standing by the lake, and the woman became another mountain, snow-capped, that lies to the south.

Some say the mountain smokes from sorrow, others say from anger.

He must be very sad today, I say in Nahuatl. The woman turns, alarmed, to see me standing next to her. I smile, hoping to dissolve the hostile panic on her face, but she grips her child's chin and turns his head away, so he does not look at me. Then she grabs him by the arm and hurries him away.

Not despondent, for, in my decades here, I have received every manner of response to my appearance, unforewarned, I continue on my way. The streets are full of puddles. Ayate fibre is being dried, blockages in over-flowing gutters are being cleared, and floating debris is being picked from the gates of high canals. The city smells of earth and stone.

Above, there circle eagles.

As I step carefully through a brown pool across the road, the tip of my shoe disturbs a limp revolving form. The mushy body of a yellow lizard, drowned, floats belly-up, its hands outstretched, its mouth set tight, like an overcooked egg yolk. Distorted eagles swim in their reflections at the lizard's tail.

The walls of the buildings crawl with multitudes of snails. Children are at work plucking the creatures from the stone, squeezing them from their shells and tossing them into piles. The lower walls have been cleared, leaving only smears of slime, and in several places now the smaller children balance on the shoulders of the taller ones, stretching up to catch the snails that have climbed to greater heights. As I watch, a little girl places one upon her tongue.

I look for marks of sickness on her but can see no signs.

Stranger, she says, gesturing at me with her thumb. The other children turn to stare and I look away. How long? I think savagely. How long until they do not stare? I have lived here twenty years, have learned their culture, speak their tongue. Since before they were born.

It will never be enough.

I walk away, thinking of the snails and their shattered shells, on towards the marketplace, which is teeming in the sunshine. Past the basket-weavers' stalls, past gourds and brightly painted jars, past copper axes, firewood, rope, fabric, mounded spices. Here the skins of rabbits are stretched to dry on wooden frames. There lie scarred cactus limbs and the soft feathers of grey owls. When we came to Tenochtitlan we were astounded at the scale of this great daily fair, vaster and better organised than any bazaar in Andalus, and at the richness of its wares. I am sometimes still astounded. Something will catch me unawares, some item of fine craftsmanship or the rainbow feathers of a bird singing in a wicker cage, or the sculpted teeth of jaguars, and wonder will wash over me. But that is not today. Today I wander in a daze, seeing the outer shapes of things but never seeing into them. A pile of seeds. Fried flying ants. A goose quill. A naked slave. I see Abd al-Wahid's eyes, as they shone on that first day.

We have found the centre of a world, he said.

It is my centre.

Now I am walking near that place where our caravan first staggered in, to display the things we had brought to a staring crowd. From our camels' sagging humps fell sacks of merchandise from half the span around the world, much of it compromised from the arduous journeys it had made. Bales of tea had rotted black. Leather was green with mould. The priceless carpet we had brought as a gift to the emperor, donated by the caliph himself from his graceful palace in Qurtubah, was discoloured from the sun and, in some parts, lousy. But the Mexica did not see these flaws, as we did not see theirs.

Soon the only thing we saw was dazzling Moctezuma.

When he stepped down from the palanquin, his people sighed. His sandal straps were set with pearls. Their soles were shod in gold. The mass of his patterned cloak spilled out like an unfurling wing, gold-hemmed, and his gorgeous headdress rose tall into the light, quetzal-feathered, shimmering green. Light seemed to flood from him. We bowed our heads and only Malinala held her steady gaze as he came on, his face aglow.

The lustre on his skin, we later learned, was powdered gold.

In Andalus there is a myth that the emperor thought we might be gods returning from across the sea, with our skins of different shades, our steeds, our noisy weapons. But we were tired, ragged, sick, bewildered in this New Maghreb.

The Mexica have never doubted which of us is mortal.

A pile of incense smouldering. Obsidian knives. Charcoal and bone. My feet, ungilded, draw me on. There is music playing somewhere. Inside this crowd, many thousands deep, I feel an ache of loneliness that is connected, in some way, to that vision of the emperor on our initial sight of him, magnificent and remote.

I am often lonely here.

In the arms of my wife, in the company of other Moors. No matter how far I have come it stalks me like a shadow. And then I think of backgammon, the black and white pieces of the games that I have played with him, the man they call the Frowning Lord, for in his eyes I see the same.

There is nothing more lonely than a god, even among gods.

As I walk I am aware of a space that opens up ahead and fills in again behind, an ambulatory emptiness maintaining the same pace as me. It stops when I stop, travels when I travel. Perhaps it is nothing but my mood, but the mushriks seem to flow away as I approach, avoiding me, displacing themselves subtly in a way I have not known before. Or perhaps I have not noticed. Has something changed? Something has changed. I glance around and see no eyes, for their eyes are turned away.

Perhaps I have imagined it.

I have imagined it.

The history of the caliphate is marked by two opposing trends that wax and wane throughout the years, tugging our fortunes after them. Abundance and austerity. Now we are in abundance. I have always found it strange that our domestic opulence, stemming from the caliph's law and from long centuries of peace, has found its full expression here, in the marketplace of another world. Tenochtitlan, I sometimes think, is what Qurtubah yearns to be.

But the abundance does not last. Austerity always follows. I think, again, of Benmessaoud, with his desert purity, his condemnation of the things upon which we have built our wealth. Of xocolatl and tubaq. Our alliance with the ungodly. After the uprising, we heard, his soldiers smashed the drinking bowls and destroyed imported goods, put smoke-drinkers to the sword, denounced the corrupting influence of this mushrik Babylon.

He does not like you, Eli, is what Mohammed Issa said.

The point is theoretical.

It is theoretical until it is put into practice.

Powdered maiz. Cactus thorns. Blankets. Turquoise beetle shells. Reed flutes. Captive animals. Feathers. Fibres. Amulets. What have I come here looking for? I cannot remember.

Down one brightly coloured aisle a woman flaps a greasy rag above a slab of purple meat to keep the hungry flies away. Another place sells spearheads. Another, honeycombs. At one stall a boy is selling Moorish charms from Andalus, decorated blue glass beads to ward against the evil eye which have become popular here. On a whim I buy one.

An official of the emperor is stalking between the rows, checking weights and measurements, preceded by a slave who bears the standard of his rank, nine golden dots on blue. I stroke the smooth bead with my thumb. Then I turn into another aisle and see Coyotl.

The messenger has his back to me but his body is distinct. The veins in his strong legs are knotted like a horse's. He is walking swiftly, his head bent low, away

from me, sliding through the crowd, powerful and pur-
poseful. I make to call after him but something holds my
tongue. Is it the dullness of his skin, the splattered stains
upon his clothes, that put me in mind of someone who has
come from far away? I do not know but I am sure he has
travelled beyond the city. This, of course, is not unusual
for a runner such as he, who might be called to carry news
over deserts and snowy mountain peaks as well as to the
nearest town, or from one street to the next. Nonetheless
I follow him. He is walking westwards.

Why have you brought me no reply? I intend to ask
him. It has almost been ten days, when normally responses
from the emperor's court are brisk and prompt. What can
be the cause of such a long delay? Not that a messenger
is privy to the business of the Black House, but whom
else can I consult? He might have heard some gossip.
Messengers hear all kinds of things, like the drivers of
our caravans, whose paths they sometimes cross on the
trade routes of this continent. So I hurry after him, following the black bowl of his hair as it weaves left and
right, bound by the white headband that indicates his
profession. The market buzzes like a hive. It is all I can do
to keep him within my sight. He turns north, then west
again, never glancing at the stalls. I lose sight of him as he
ducks beneath an awning. He is briefly lost and then I find
him again beside the crumbled western wall, the boundary of the marketplace. He passes beneath the lintels of
the covered walkway.

Here is a place where peasants sell a drink made
from fermented grain, not as strong as cactus wine but

nonetheless intoxicating. Around this stall, white-robed figures gather like moths. They wear no skullcaps on their heads, but I see, to my surprise, that they are Mexica converts, six or seven of them. I wonder what the imam would say to see them here. Coyotl has briefly joined this crowd and is standing next to one who is taller than the rest, robed in grey rather than white. But his features are not Mexica. A narrow face. A shaven lip. It is that fellow Hasan.

The incident does not last long, and if I had not been watching closely I would not have seen a thing. But it seems to me that for a moment the two men confer. Their heads dip towards one another, as if in confidence, and Coyotl moves his lips. Hasan briefly nods. Then Coyotl is on his way, passing from the marketplace into the broad streets beyond, and as I pause to watch him go, Hasan turns to greet me.

Ambassador to the Sun, he says, smiling. Peace be with you.

And with you, I say.

At last it has stopped, he says.

What has stopped?

That bitter rain. They say it was quite unseasonable. I hope that, at your age, you did not catch a chill?

His eyes are clouded with concern. Again there is no mockery. He seems to wish the best for me.

I caught no chill, I say.

God willing you will have good health, he says, smiling amiably.

God willing we all will, I say.

What would the Moorish Quarter be without its dhimmi?

I open my mouth to speak and close it, not knowing what to say. The question seems innocent, even well intentioned.

What brings you here? he asks, apparently not noticing. He gestures vaguely at the stall where the converts loiter.

The usual affairs, I say. I have business everywhere. You keep unusual company.

They are not with me, he says.

It is so obviously a lie that I almost challenge him, for I saw him standing with these men and he knows that I saw. But of course I have no proof. He would only have to say so. His easy words inhibit me from mentioning the messenger, which I had a mind to do, for he could deny that too. Instead I ask, What brings you here? echoing his own question.

The wonders of this city, he says in a tone that is rapturous, a tone that, following his lie, shocks me with its innocence. He spreads his arms out wide and beams. Is it not a marvel?

It is many things, I say, unprepared for this turn, as I am unprepared for almost everything about this man. He reminds me of a quetzal feather that alters colour as it turns, one moment green, one moment blue. At the same time bright and dark. It is many things, I say. A marvel is one of them.

Well, I am a newcomer. You have been here a long time. Perhaps the gold has lost its shine for you.

Most things do, I say.

But it might be that some things shine even more, he says. Things that were dull before.

I make no reply, for I do not know what he means. Every word that he speaks has another word behind it.

Scratching at his greyish shaven lip with a lazy hand, he says, I am curious. In Andalus they talk of you. Ever since I was a boy I was familiar with your name.

You are still a boy, is what I want to say. Instead I wait to see what comes.

I often wondered how it was, he says. On the founding fleet. When you came across the sea, not knowing what was on the other side. If there was another side.

It was rough. I was sick. Now I am here.

He waits. I give him nothing more. A smile spreads across his face.

Now you are here. Now I am here. Now all of us are here, he says, and more to follow after us. Will we ever see home again?

This is my home, I say.

There is a commotion as a man leading ducks on strings loses control of his birds, which shriek and flap about. The mushrik scurries after them, grabbing at their long necks. Laughing onlookers look on. The converts observe silently, cradling their forbidden cups. Hasan watches briefly and turns back to me. When I was a boy, he says, I used to wonder how you knew.

Knew what? I say.

To cross the sea. They say you heard it in a dream.

Do they indeed? I say.

The story that I heard is that God spoke to you, that he sent an angel with flaming wings, a golden face. That the angel pointed west. That the caliph granted you a fleet.

Believe it if you like, I say. It is a pretty story.

I would like to hear your story, even if it is not pretty. I would be most interested.

The ducks have been retethered on their strings and the man pulls them away. They follow him with loud complaints. Soon they will have their necks cut and their feathers pulled out.

One of the mushrik converts spits.

A dancer weaves through the crowd, masked like a crocodile.

There are enough stories for you here, I say. In this city of wonders.

He regards me for a time then rubs his hands together, pleased. You are a busy man, he says, so I will say good day to you. Or, as the mushriks say, good sun.

You speak a little Nahuatl?

Only a few small words. Maybe you could teach me.

It would be my pleasure, I say, telling an untruth of my own. Well, with peace, I add.

With peace, he says. Then he says, The angel with the burning wings. Of course I never believed that tale, but it causes me to think. Might others, who come here after you, not themselves be sent by God?

Already his back is turned on me and he does not linger by the stall but goes abruptly down an aisle and is lost from sight. The man might never have been here.

Would that he were not.

*　　*　　*

And now, because of him, I am back in Qadis. The great port of the caliphate, from which, each day, a hundred ships set sail and a hundred ships return, from every point around the world. Its harbour always full of sails, its sky raucous with gulls. I can see the cobbled lane that runs uphill from the wharf, can see my shoes upon the stones, heel-worn and holey. Before I dreamed to cross the sea. Before I was who I am. Ahead there was a synagogue but before I came to it there was a narrow door, a teahouse where the merchants went to trade their news of distant storms, treasure fleets, Christian pirates, cargos lost and evil winds. I stepped inside there on a whim, having no other place to go.

Was there some hand at my back? No, I do not think so. Did someone mutter in my ear? It was not the voice of God. In a corner there he sat, no angel with a glowing face but just a curly-headed drunk, a Christian, a foreigner, scowling into his wine. I took the table next to him because no one else would sit there.

I shake the memory away, like so many times before. My mind goes to the papers in the iron chest in my quarters. It has been years since I looked at them, those calculations written in his untidy, sloping hand, those fragments of seeming gibberish. They have no purpose now. I should have tossed them in the sea the moment that we came to land, where silver fish and starfish would soon have nibbled them away.

Perhaps I will burn them after all, with that sick child's lock of hair.

The north side of the marketplace is bounded by the court of games, where the uli-sellers were. They are nowhere to be seen now. Some pine sticks and a green rag is all that is left of them, their stall dismantled and removed.

Gone, says a seller of pots who squats nearby with his wares, when I greet him to enquire. Back to their country in the south. Two nights ago they went away.

Why? I ask. But his face turns dense, in that way I have come to recognise.

No matter. It is a little thing. But it makes me wary.

As I walk through the Caliph's Gate, Coyotl is on his way back out. The message has come for you, he says. I gave it to the lady.

You must be paid, I say, startled at the sight of him.

The Woman of the Knots has paid. Our business is concluded.

I am obliged. Did your feet... did your feet take you far? I ask, trying to recall the formal phrasing of his guild.

The Lord of Winds carried me, he says, which is not an answer.

I should ask about Hasan, but I miss my opportunity. My mind is still back in the teahouse in Qadis. So the messenger slips away, walking not-fast and yet fast in that way he seems to have, and I go to my quarters, where my wife is boiling water.

Did you bring amaranth? she asks.

Ah, it must have slipped my mind, I say, remembering only then what it was I went to the market for.

Foolish one, she says, but she says it kindly.

I bought this trinket, I say, showing her the blue glass bead. Would you like to wear it? It keeps away the evil eye.

I have no need of that, she says. Look, a message has come for you.

Her eyes indicate my desk. Now her voice is not so kind.

I paid the messenger, she says. But it is not my business.

Did you feed my pet to the hairless dog? I have an impulse to demand. Was that your punishment for what Abd al-Wahid asked of me?

But I do not say anything.

Peace is built on silence.

Instead I go to my desk to unfurl the parchment scroll, embellished with a blazing sun and the emblems of the emperor. There is a house whose walls are black, the day-sign 11 Deer and the week-sign 1 Snake, a date five days from now. Then a glyph denoting speech and two circles, one black, one white.

Again my finger strokes the charm. Against the evil eye.

The Third Sun was the Lord of Rain, Malinala tells me later as we lie together.

Not lie together, I should say, in the manner that we did before, when our love was vigorous. But lie together side by side.

At times I wish for more.

The Lord of Rain was fierce, she says, with the sharp teeth of a jaguar. With his axe he struck the clouds to make the thunder growl. His brother, who only had one foot, the Smoking Mirror, watched from below. He dreamed of taking his revenge. The Smoking Mirror was always jealous.

At times I wish for more but for now this is enough, our bodies touching at three points, at our elbows, fingers, toes. Skin on skin, our blood below, our organs working in the dark. We have lain like this for twenty years. We must love one another.

As the Smoking Mirror watched, she says, he saw his brother's wife walk by, She of the Jade-Green Skirt. And what happened then?

Her question takes me by surprise.

What happened? I ask.

You know, she says. You can tell it for a change.

Her body shifts on the bed and her hip touches mine. Four points. For now, it is enough.

Let me think, I say.

When She of the Jade-Green Skirt walked by, the Smoking Mirror desired her, I say, remembering the tale from the times I have heard it told before. So the Smoking Mirror carried her away and took her for his own, which caused the Lord of Rain such grief that the rain stopped falling.

And what happened then, my ugly deer? she says, moving once again. Her cool toes shift away from mine, and her elbow shifts as well. Three points. Two points.

There was drought. The plants died. The animals died. Men were in despair, I say. They prayed desperately for rain.

And did the Lord of Rain send rain?

No, he sent down fire.

Yes, he sent down fire, she says, her voice gentle in the dark. Everything was burned away. The plants, the animals, the men, the mountains, the lakes and seas. Then the sky went black again.

One point. Only our fingers touch, my little finger and her thumb.

That was the end of the Third Sun, when the world was filled with flames.

In the morning I awake to noises of confusion.

Voices shouting in the yard. Footsteps scuffing back and forth. A donkey braying pointlessly.

Malinala is not here.

My door crashes open.

Mohammed Issa is standing there, half dressed in the day's half-light. Eli, he cries, you must come. Then he has a fit of coughing.

By the time his husky sobs have eased I am across the room, struggling into my shoes, though I do not know what I need them for.

Issa's voice is cracked and raw.

It is the caravan, he says. The caravan is destroyed.

· SIX ·

I T was the godless Chichimecs!
No Chichimecs could do this thing. They are scaven-
gers, not warriors.

Where did the outrage take place?

It was not Tlaxcalans, then?

Tlaxcala would not wage war on us.

They would wage war on Mexica.

A sacrilege!

Was it him?

They would but they cannot. Their city is not strong
enough.

How many survived? How many beasts?

My gold!

I tell you, it was there. Where the river meets that
steep ravine, the ambush must have happened there. Have
I not often warned...?

Three thousand dirhams, more.

Maybe it was Zapotecs.

Was it him? It was him!

Zapotecs? Impossible.

Six thousand dirhams.

Tortoiseshell! Eighteen crates of uncut jade!

How many survived?

Slaughtered, all. The camels and the horses too...

I have often warned of the danger there, but no one listened. That ravine...

The work of evil spirits, djinns!

Peace! Everybody, peace!

Only two weeks' march from here...

In the shadowed valleys of those hills, I have always said...

Surely some of them survived.

Were they asleep on camelback?

Peace, for the love of God!

Why were there not more guards?

From where I sit, on the broken fountain's lip, in the shade of the crooked olive tree that was planted long ago but which has still not reached my height, and which has never borne one fruit, I watch the Moors of the Moorish Quarter surging like a stormy sea. Angry, frightened, scandalised, excited, outraged, merely stunned, men are dashing here and there debating and petitioning, assembling and dividing according to their arguments. In their midst Abd al-Wahid braces himself solidly, like someone trying to hold position in a roaring current.

Fellows, please! Order, peace! he cries, but no one heeds his words.

Zapotecs! yells the Riffish carpet-seller, discounted though his theory is.

It is a punishment from God!

Did they not have arquebuses?

I have lost everything!

Could the Franks have landed here?

Absurd.

Who else could it be but him?

We must send help. Those that survived...

The finest tubaq!

None survived.

Between the brown plains and the sea...

We must respond!

Everything...

Eli! What do you say? Why are you just sitting there?

This spot is comfortable, I say. And I do not know what else to do.

But what is in your mind?

Nothing is in my mind, I say.

In truth what is in my mind is a sense of similarity, a feeling that this scene has unfolded recently, in some other thing I have seen. The frantic movement back and forth. The mindless agitation. It bothers me, a memory in the corner of my thoughts, and all I wish to do is to sit here with my eyes half closed, to let the image find itself.

A merchant hurries close to me clutching something in his arms protectively, as if pursued, an absurd expression on his face. With that the picture comes to me.

The black ants in their broken nest. The teeming of the eggs.

Who brought the news? I ask the man who was standing

over me, but he has moved away to flap his mouth at some-one else.

Still not knowing what to do, I clamber to my feet.

Occasionally our caravans were assaulted in the early years, as they passed by hostile towns or strayed into the territories of those who did not wish Moors well. We suffered ambush and betrayal, with men and riches lost. But for the most part such attacks were repulsed by arquebus fire, the malefactors chased away and trampled by our cavalry, for, in those uncertain times, our routes were better guarded. Then Moctezuma made it known that the Moors of Tenochtitlan were his invited guests and friends, that insults visited on us were insults visited on him. Offending cities were besieged, their fields of maiz burned down, and eagle knights and jaguar knights marched the evildoers back to meet their ends on the temple steps. So justice, of a kind, was done.

Since then our caravans have been happily unmolested.

If this ugly thing is true, then this attack is something new.

I calculate what I might have lost.

A fortune in dark beans.

Forty packs on forty beasts, marked with the sigil of my house. They pass before my eyes, swaying one by one. Was it him? It must be him. But it is too loud to think. Through my milling countrymen I insinuate my way, evading hands upon my sleeve and foolish questions and demands, until I have crossed the yard. I need space and quiet. My desire for these qualities, in addition, I realise now, to the recollection of the ants and of whose small hands prised up the stone, has brought me to the mosque. Kicking off my shoes, I enter.

The mosque is empty but feels full, as if the dome's upended bowl does not contain a vacancy but instead a solid form, a weight of air pressing down. Where is the god? asked the emperor's men when they first came to this place. The gods of the Mexica have faces, fingers, tongues and toes, displays of corporeality as vulgar as the fleshly, bloodied idols that are flaunted in the churches of the Christians. Our Moorish God is without form. But still I feel His weight.

Not wishing to linger long, for fear of discovery, I cross the floor and hurry to the place where I put the hair. Tweaking back the carpet's hem reveals a bare stone floor. There is nothing underneath. The knot of hair has gone.

Lord, I say, glancing up.

I let the carpet fall.

Lord, I attempt again.

But nothing is forthcoming.

An entire caravan! Surely it cannot be so. Six hundred camels, a baggage train that stretched for mile after mile. It is not possible.

What happened to the hair?

As I blunder out again, my hands clutching at themselves in distress I did not feel outside amidst so much other distress, I walk into the imam who is coming the other way.

What are you doing here? he asks.

I came for peace, I say.

The imam has, I have always thought, a strangely melted quality, like a stick of candle wax that has softened and reformed. His cheeks and chin are soft and slumped, as is the rest of his face, pale and aqueous. Only his eyes are hard.

You have your synagogue for that, he says.

It is here too, I say.

He takes a breath, as if to scold me with some point of the caliph's law, then suddenly, surprisingly, his eyes turn soft like the rest of him and I imagine with a shock that he is about to cry. His hand goes briefly to his face and his body rocks. Should I comfort him? I wonder. The thing is hard to contemplate, for this man has always been so rude and hostile to me.

I partway extend my hand, which does not quite cross the space but halts between us in the air, like an unconcluded bridge.

It is an evil day, he says. Those poor Muslims. Those poor men. Who did this thing, Eli?

When his eyes turn back to me they have gone hard again.

I do not know, I say. We will find out before long.

He glances at my hand. It looks foolish hanging there, so I lower it uncomfortably.

Your converts are drinking alcohol, I want to say to him.

I will go, I say instead. With peace.

The imam only nods.

I spend too long a time outside fumbling with my shoes.

*　　*　　*

How did this awful news arrive? Not one person seems to know. The knowledge has simply manifested, fully formed, between these walls, as if it has been jointly dreamed. It has gathered shape out of the air like a revelation.

A lone survivor staggered back, answers one man when I ask. He had arrows in his back. He died, I think. He must have died.

A mushrik runner brought the news, answers someone else.

A conference of some description is taking place inside the gate, with some fellow standing on a crate waggling his arms. I do not need to listen long before knowing that it is nonsense. Conjecture. Hearsay. Useless words. Other men are shouting, but I recognise almost none of them. Their faces are like those of boys. How did they come to be here and to hold such opinions?

There is no guard at the gate, which seems especially negligent, and curious Mexica faces are peering through the entranceway. One white-cloaked man I recognise, one of Issa's merchant friends, is leaning on a long staff, his features solemn and detached. Three priests of the Feathered Serpent stand together looking on, draped in green embroidered robes. They are chewing popped maiz. This must mean war! shouts someone. Thinking that perhaps another conference is going on, a meeting of older, wiser heads, of which I have not been informed, I struggle through the crowd again towards Abd al-Wahid's quarters.

This must mean war. But with whom? And how would we prosecute it? In the early days of our settlement a cavalry was stabled here, with soldiers of the caliphate and cannons mounted at the gate. But those days have gone now. Our armoury holds arquebuses, but few of us have any skill in their loading or their firing, which is a complicated task. We are men of trade, not war. Now Moctezuma is our sword and he is our shield as well.

The crescent moon inside the sun. The symbol of our quarter.

Abd al-Wahid's private rooms are situated at the other end of the Moorish Quarter from my own, and occupy two floors of what was once a summer house for some of the emperor's cousins, now fallen out of favour. Its latticed windows, at the back, look eastwards across the lake. The breeze is fresher on that side, away from the bad airs of the city. It even has a watergate where Abd al-Wahid keeps a boat, though he never uses it, and he lives here alone, though he has a mushrik mistress.

The door is closed. I rap the wood and wait, but there is no reply. In the cause of urgency I push the door ajar. Everything looks much the same as the last time I visited, the furnished room a testament to the wealth its owner has accrued. There are rich coverings on the walls, of designs both Moorish and Mexica. In one corner hangs a sword in a bejewelled scabbard. Three-legged wooden chairs are placed around a water-pipe, and the floor is carpeted. There is a head upon the floor.

My eyes travel back again.

There is a head upon the floor.

I take a step into the room and close the door behind me.

The head is simply sitting there. Can heads be said to sit? I approach it cautiously, from a three-quarter profile, avoiding a frontal advance. Its eyes are not quite closed. It is not a head, I observe as I come close to it, of any great significance, not a head of anyone I know. It is recognisably a Moor. Its face is young and sad. Its tender beard appears, it seems, to have been partly burned away, for the curly black-ish hair is missing on one side. Its lips and ears are delicate.

An ordinary head.

Of course I have seen heads before, detached from their supporting necks. Heads of rebels in Andalus, of criminals and adulterers, heads of mushriks harvested in the Flower War. I have seen the flensing-house where such heads are scraped and boiled, defleshed, bound for the Rack of Skulls. I am not shocked by this head. But its presence is surprising.

I tap it carefully with my shoe. Its cheek feels hard, like wood. It wobbles gently on its stump.

Whose head is that? I ask myself. The question makes me laugh.

I can hear Malinala's voice as if she were inside the room. It is no one's head, she says.

It is all our heads, I say.

A thump, and I turn to see Abd al-Wahid in the door, an aghast expression on his face. I realise, troubled, that I spoke those words aloud. Abd al-Wahid stares at me as if it were not the severed head, but rather I, intact and whole, that was the disturbing presence here. His eyeballs bulge. Sweat beads and runs from the big pores of his face. What are you doing here? he asks.

What is this head doing here? I ask.

Someone yells his name outside.

Go away! he bellows.

He pauses as if taking stock, then steps inside and slams the door. It is chaos out there, he says. It is embarrassing. Let us have a bit of peace. A moment. Will you please sit down? Does anyone know that you are here?

About this head... I say.

Yes, we will come to that. What are you doing in my house? I could have you disciplined.

You could not have me disciplined, I say.

You are right, I could not. And of course I would not wish to. Eli, will you not sit down? I am feeling somewhat weak. A moment, that is all I need.

I am your guest, I say.

We sit upon respective chairs, the head between us on the floor. From this angle I can only see an orb of hair. The hair is dirty, specked with dust, and looks as if it has been wet. It is the unwashed hair of one who has travelled a long road.

He was from the caravan? I ask.

Abd al-Wahid says, So I assume. Not a camel-driver, though. I surely know them all by sight. Perhaps he was a muleteer. He must have set out with the rest of them.

And how did he... get back again?

I found him here. It here.

Abd al-Wahid heaves a sigh and fiddles with his jewellery. He has always been a man for vanities and adornments. Each of his fingers wears a ring, and a pendant hangs around his neck. One pearl-set ring revolves around one finger like a prayer-bead.

It was on my doorstep when I got up for the morning prayer, he says. I almost trod on it. I carried it inside. It came in this, he says, holding up a cotton bag spotted with brown stains.

Was there nothing else? I ask.

Just these, says Abd al-Wahid.

His hand delves into the bag and re-emerges as a fist. The fist unclenches, pink inside, like the opening of a shell. In his palm are two things, or two categories of thing. Some crumbled shreds of tubaq leaves and some xocolatl beans.

So, I say. It was him.

So it would appear, he says.

This is a warning, then, I say.

It is an intention.

He brings his full palm to his face and inhales professionally. Last season's harvest, he says. Then he shuts his fist. Abd al-Wahid, the head and I sit together quietly, three points of a skewed and intimate trigonometry, while the uproar of the Moorish Quarter falls and rises.

Have any of the others seen? I ask eventually.

I have shown no one, he says. I was deciding what to do.

Then how do they all know the news?

I do not understand it. When I went to the mosque some people were assembled there, clamouring as they are now. Some said this and some said that. No one knows who told it first. Everyone talks of an attack but they tell it different ways, so that it makes no sense at all. The thing is like a ball of snakes. I cannot find the end of it.

Like the stories of my wife, I say. They never stay the same but change with every telling. Sometimes She of the Jade-Green Skirt is raped, sometimes she falls in love. Sometimes men are turned into monkeys, sometimes other beasts. But their meaning stays the same...

What are you talking about? he yells. I have no time for your nonsense now! In God's name, will you concentrate?

My apologies, I say.

This is what we know, he says, mopping at his shining brow. Disturbing news has come to us. We do not know its provenance. We do, however, have this head, which someone has delivered to us. We do not know whose head it is, but we know, or we believe, that it comes from the caravan, which that fanatic from the sands has ambushed and perhaps destroyed. In order to disrupt our trade. In order to prevent mushrik goods from reaching Andalus. These leaves and beans are his sign. At the least, we can surmise...

Yes, I say, nodding sagely to each point he makes. But I find it difficult to focus on his words. My mind is not in the room but, as seems to be occurring more and more frequently of late, I am thinking of the story Malinala told last night, or the story that she made me tell. When the Third Sun ended and the world expired in drought. The thirsty people prayed for rain but their god sent down fire. They begged for water and got flames. Everything was burned away.

Everything was burned away, but in another version of the tale some men survived. Some became huehxolotl-birds and some became butterflies. Some became hairless dogs, which are recognised as the brothers of men and the children of the evening star, wretched creatures though they are.

Did all men die? Did some survive? It is a ball of snakes.

We will send out cavalry, Abd al-Wahid is saying, to ascertain what has occurred.

We do not have cavalry, I say. They went with the caravan.

We have horses, we have men. We must send them down the road. They will ride like the wind.

God willing, I say.

Tell me, Eli, tell me that the Frowning Lord has sent for you. Surely you have heard by now.

We will meet in four days' time, I say.

Four days? It is too long. He must sink the floating roads so that Benmessaoud cannot cross the lake. He must send his feathered knights...

It is all we have, I say.

Abd al-Wahid heaves a sigh. He sits there with his big legs splayed. His chair is much too small for him.

There is something else, I say.

The pearly ring goes round and round.

This sickness.

Abd al-Wahid groans.

I know you know that it is here, I say. It is in the neighbourhoods. The mushriks are aware of it. Some have already left Tenochtitlan. The uli-sellers, the Mayayans, they departed days ago. They have seen these signs before...

But Abd al-Wahid cuts me off with a sweep of his great gleaming hand, an action that reminds me of the guard bringing down his scimitar. We will not speak of this, he says. There is nothing we can do. Such things are the will of God.

You talk like someone else, I say.

What is that supposed to mean?

He glares at me suspiciously, but before any more is said there is pounding on the door, and voices calling out his name.

I will attend! he bellows.

He draws himself to his feet, then totters and slumps down again. The glare is gone from his face.

What of the head? he says. No one else must see it yet. It will only further panic them. Here, put this over it.

He plucks the bag from the floor and tosses it at me. It flops, sagging, on my knee.

Hurry, man, he says.

The bag is soft and dry. It has a faint smell of mushrooms. When I turn it upside down some crumbled tubaq leaves drift down, like ash or snow, upon the head, settling on the matted hair. I drop the bag over the head and pull the drawstring tight.

That will have to do, says Abd al-Wahid. Leave it there for now. There are many things to organise. There are idiots to shout at me. Go, Eli. Go in peace. We shall see each other later.

When I open the door a gaggle of men stands outside, flush-faced from whatever debate they have been engaged in. They peer into the room, glaring at me as if I were an impediment or obstacle. Is the Chief Vizier inside? shouts one.

He is on his way, I say.

*　　*　　*

Out I stroll into the crowd. Men are still dashing here and there, but with diminished urgency. Some are sitting on their own, thoughtful, as I was doing. One is making rapid calculations on an abacus. Outside the stables, a harelipped groom manhandles a grey mule.

I am making for my rooms, but scarcely have I walked ten steps before a hand claps on my arm. To my consternation it is Abd al-Wahid again. His face looms close to mine and he whispers violently, as if, by hissing like a snake, no one will see us standing here, in the middle of the crowd, when he is in such great demand. Take it! he says.

Something is thrust into my arms, something round and heavy. The object has been wrapped in a brightly coloured rug. I attempt to push it back but he is more forceful than me, and there are people watching us. Reluctantly my hands accept.

You must take it, he says. Take it to the emperor.

What does the emperor want with it?

Use it to frighten him.

If ever a man were to be frightened of a head, I say, it would not be him. I do not think...

Chief Vizier! cries a man from the delegation at the door. We beseech your company!

I am coming! shouts Abd al-Wahid. Then he says between his teeth, Eli, do not cause a scene.

It is not I...

For the love of God! Do not show it to your wife. Do not let the other merchants see. Now go. Yes, I am coming! he yells.

Then he turns his broad back and quickly walks away.

Eli Ben Abram, have you heard? asks a passing man, his eyes full of fear and glee. The caravan! Your fortune, lost! What is it that you have there?

I turn my back on him, though it is not so broad.

Some became huehxolotl-birds, some butterflies, some hairless dogs. Most, perhaps, became hairless dogs. I bear the lump towards my rooms like an item from the market.

From the place of willow trees we watch the horsemen depart at a gallop down the floating road, which shudders with their hoofbeats. There are only three of them. They are scouts, not cavalrymen. One brandishes a slender pole from which a green banner streams, and his turban-cloth streams too, snapping backwards with the wind, and as they reach the middle of the lake this banner-waving man lets out an ululating cry that carries faintly back to us. A sight of small magnificence, I think as I watch them go. Diminishing and diminishing as they storm across the lake, they become very small against the vast landscape. The nearest hills, which have the shape of wedges, are dim and grey, while the higher peaks beyond are lost in smudgy cloud. The smoking mountain, quiet today, says nothing. The warrior does not weep.

Come, says Malinala, tweaking at my elbow.

A sight of small magnificence, but their start was not propitious. There was an incident as they left the Moorish Quarter. As the horses were prepared, one roan, one chestnut and one grey, and as the three men packed supplies, a small crowd formed to watch them go. Mushriks gathered at the gate, as they are inclined to do when there is a spectacle, especially one that involves swift deer. Even after twenty years they are still amazed to see them. The riders mounted, spurred their steeds, then proceeded one by one at a brisk trot through the Caliph's Gate. God be with you! someone called as they passed beneath the archway.

It was too fast to see, and I only caught the edge of it. An object wheeling through the air from the gathered Mexica. It hit the grey horse on the rump, the animal took fright and reared, and its rider, unprepared, was pitched into the dust. The mushriks scattered with loud cries as the horse stampeded through the crowd, dragging the poor man after it by one foot that he could not free, until the rider of the roan caught the scared brute by the reins.

It was over quickly and the man was not badly hurt, only scraped and filthy from his contact with the road. As the horsemen reconvened, angry, back inside the gate, someone grabbed my elbow for the second time that day.

The son of a whore has been caught! cried the guard with the Frankish knife. His spittle rained upon my face.

The son of which whore? I asked.

Two more guards, the one who chews the root and another one, were struggling with a mushrik man, holding him roughly by the arms.

What shall we do with him? they asked as I approached.

What was it that he threw? I asked.

Some filthy vegetable, one said.

A vegetable?

We should cut off his hands!

You will do no such thing, I said. Let me speak with him. Hold him still so I can speak. You! What is your name?

The man's face turned to me at the sound of Nahuatl, but I knew from a glance that he was an imbecile. A string of drool hung from his mouth and his eyes were dusty. I had seen more intelligence in the eyes of the startled horses.

Nonetheless I persevered. Why did you insult those Moors, the riders of the swift deer? I asked. It was dishonourable. Between our people there is peace. My caliph and your emperor.

He should be whipped! cried the thick-necked guard.

Quiet now, I said.

See them run, said the mushrik in a clotted voice.

What does he say? asked the guard.

I said quiet! I said.

See the swift deer run, the man said. Then he threw back his head and made a whinnying sound.

He is mad, I told the guards. Let him go. He means no harm.

He attacked our horses...

With a vegetable, I said.

The third guard, whom I did not know, rounded on me with a sneer. What authority do you have? he asked.

I drew my breath.

I am Ambassador to the Sun, I told him in a level voice. Without me you would not be here. None of this would be here. I have the ear of Abd al-Wahid. I could have you disciplined. I have the ear of the emperor too. If I wished,

I could have you dragged up those temple steps. Now let him go, as I command. We will speak no more of this.

Once released, the idiot stumbled off into the crowd.

Groups of surrounding Mexica had been watching this unfold, chattering excitedly. They began to drift away. Issa's friend, the merchant with the topknot and the blue-hemmed cloak, turned without acknowledging me. One onlooker, as she left, stooped to pluck the offending missile from the spot on which it lay, tucking it inside her dress.

A battered cob of maiz.

Touched by the Lord of Rain, that is what the mushrik priests would say. The Lord of Rain, among other things, is the god of imbecility. That fellow will be punished, perhaps, for his troublemaking act, but if he is, it will be by his people and not by us.

Such incidents are not unknown in the history of our quarter. The scales are delicately set and occasionally they have tipped. There have been skirmishes, fist fights, even minor riots. Long ago fifteen Mexica were killed by arquebus fire. But we have survived all that. The peace between us has survived. The hurling of a maiz cob by a madman is a small affair.

It makes another ripple, though. And sometimes ripples overlap.

I should not have said that thing about the temple steps.

All of that happened hours ago, in the middle of the day. The crowd has gone, the valiant horsemen have passed down the floating road, and Malinala takes my hand as we walk back to the city gate. The tumult of the early morning feels dim and far away, cloudy, like the distant hills. It is afternoon. Now I am tired.

The head. The head wrapped in its rug.

I should not have said that thing about the temple steps.

How long?

Familiar homely sounds. The beans clatter in the pan.

Too long.

The hiss of steam. The dance of boiling water.

How long now?

That sweet-dark fragrance billowing across the room.

Long enough.

She is at my side. The cup is at my mouth.

The xocolatl hits me with unusual potency tonight. It rushes up around my ears. My heart jumps to meet it. From behind my eyelids thick darkness surges everywhere, in black waves, bearing me along. Wonderful. It is wonderful. I would not live without it.

We have not spoken much about the matters of the day. About the men who are likely slain. The fortune we have lost. We have exchanged but several words, for there is nothing much to say. We do not know anything. It is a smoking mirror.

The Smoking Mirror is the god of the night sky and prophecy, the vengeful one-footed one who burned as the First Sun. And smoking mirror is also what the Mexica call obsidian, when polished to its night-black sheen. The stone of divination. Philosophising Moctezuma has on occasion pondered this while I am in his company, after a backgammon game, for it is the kind of thing that suits our conversations then, when cactus wine has been consumed and the fire is burning low. I am a mirror to my people, he has informed me more than once. An emperor sees and is yet seen. He must reflect and yet absorb.

And must he also smoke? I asked.

With tubaq streaming from his nose, he laughed. Yes, he must smoke!

That time he made a joke of it, but the Frowning Lord fears it too. For the smoking mirror is a window to other worlds. As sorcerers in the Frankish lands are said to study crystal balls, which reveal glimpses into things that have not yet come to pass, so mirrors of obsidian are fathomed by the augurs here for the inky visions they contain. But inside them there is smoke. The smoke obscures and obfuscates the bright, reflective clarity of the blackly polished stone, muddling both dark and light. The truth is only dimly glimpsed, distorted, wreathed in fog.

This is why I say this night is like a smoking mirror.

Our dreams are smoke, our truths are smoke, Moctezuma has also said, with the fire burned to ash and the cactus wine all gone.

This world is nothing but a dream.

I have never remembered dreams.

Normally I refrain from taking xocolatl at night, for it interrupts my sleep. But today is all upside down. It is past the evening prayer and I am on my second cup, for my body and my mind have much need of comfort. The day has passed confusedly, one incident after the next, leaving me with images like glyphs stacked in the codices. A crowd. A scattering of beans. A frightened horse. A maiz cob. A head. A head wrapped in a rug. My wife.

Always my wife.

Always she is here for me, beside me, near and yet far. Tonight she has been close to me. Her eyes have been watchful. She heard the news, she says, at dawn, upon returning from the lake, the shore of which she sometimes walks when she wakes early from her sleep. A passing stranger told it. Moor or Mexica? I asked. But she said it did not matter.

Why did you not come to me immediately? I demanded, but the question angered her.

You have made it clear to me where my business starts and ends, she said, you and Abd al-Wahid and the Old Men of the Nose. I should only cook and clean your robes like any Moorish wife.

Like any Mexica wife, I said.

I am not Mexica!

Her voice was jagged and abrupt, an unexpected knife. It was as if her skin had slipped and suddenly, underneath, shone hatred, raw and exposed. The sight startled me but it did not last. Within a second it had passed and then her face was hers again.

You are my heart, I said.

I was once your mouth, she said.

You are still my mouth.

But what are you to me? she said, and turned herself away.

Something happens when my wife is angry, I am ashamed to say. My countrymen would mock. The Mexica would mock. A vapour rises inside my mind, a nebulosity, turning black and white things grey, clouding everything. It confounds my clarity.

I cannot see her any more.

My wife, the smoking mirror.

I am your man of dust, I said, attempting to reach out for her.

What need have I of dust? she said.

I am your man of maiz, then.

No, you are not maiz.

Once, twice, three times she pushed my reaching hands away, and then she permitted them to bridge the void. I held her. Her eyes reflected two of me, crouching, bearded, in two inky pools of night. There were no stars. There was no light.

Then Malinala kissed me.

The caravan, she said, when her face had drawn away. I am sorry for your loss.

If it is true, I said. My voice sounded old and dry.

If it is true, she said.

Our dreams are smoke. Our truths are smoke. This is what was in my mind.

Our loss, I said.

Our loss, she said.

Then she made xocolatl.

And now I lie here comfortably, savouring the sense of it, my mouth faintly tingling from the burn of the chilli pods, while my wife lies next to me. The two of us lie together. A single candle burns low, soon to gutter in its wax, and in the dimness of the room her shoulders, bare, glow soft and warm. For now, nothing else exists. For a lustful instant I have an urge to lick them. To lick her arms, her back, her feet. To draw her body to my own. It has been a long time since I have done a thing like that.

The two of us lie together. Not in the way we did before.

The head is stuffed inside the iron chest where I keep those papers.

No angel with a glowing face but just a curly-headed drunk, a Christian, a foreigner, scowling into his wine. I took the table next to him because no one else would sit there. The conversation of the sailors and merchants in the teahouse dimmed as faces turned to look at us, a dhimmi and a foreigner, two strangers sitting side by side. Then chatter refilled the room. I ordered bread and tea. My neighbour studied me with eyes that were troubled, brown, intelligent, faintly hostile. Then they plunged away again.

His cup of wine, frowned upon, rested on a document. A paper scrawled with diagrams.

I saw a sphere. A scribbled sea.

Now the vision is obscured, as if by smoke. As if by dreams.

But it was not a dream.

· SEVEN ·

First the water turned to blood. Then came hordes of frogs. Then came lice.

Was it lice?

Then came biting flies, I think.

Then pestilence. Then weeping boils. Then storms of fire. Then locust swarms. Then came three days of night.

After those three days of night there came the sickness.

The sickness swept across the land, killing every first-born son. But God had told the chosen ones to smear their doors with lamb's blood. The four-faced Angel of Death passed by, beating his four thousand wings, and saw the signs upon their doors. The houses of the Israelites were spared.

All others died.

Was it biting flies or wild beasts? I remember differ-ent tellings. On the road, to pass the time, or resting in a caravanserai between two towns, once we had dined, or in the quiet hour before sleep, my father would sometimes tell me tales. I remember pieces of them. His stories came from the Torah, and from the One Thousand and One Nights, and from the outlandish legends of the Franks. Tales he had picked up here and there, as I have picked up mine. As my wife has picked up hers. He was not a learned man, and he mixed up their meanings.

First the water turned to blood. That was how it happened. God touched the surface of the Nile and the water boiled red. All the fishes died. The river stank, that sweet-sick stench that hangs upon the idols of this city, that clings to the temple steps, a smell I recognise too well. Egypt's water turned to blood and nobody could drink it.

It is three days since the news arrived, the news that has changed everything. Three days since the riders galloped down the floating road. Still no one knows about the head, the message sent by Benmessaoud. The theories grow fantastical. The Moors are in confusion.

Then frogs. The water teemed with frogs. They rose like bloody bubbles. Out into the fields they came, countless multitudes of them, creeping into people's homes. They swarmed inside the temples. The golden palace of the pharaoh was befouled with their slime. They clambered over everything. The land was overrun.

It is three days since the news arrived, and still no one knows anything. But this is not the only news that troubles the Moorish Quarter. Other news has come to us that keeps coming every hour, sometimes in ripples, sometimes waves, lapping like a tide. Unlike the news of the caravan, the origin of which we still have not been able to ascertain, despite the efforts of Abd al-Wahid, the merchants' council or myself, this other news is not hearsay or speculation. Rather, it is plain to see, for it is happening at our door.

Mushriks are dying in Tenochtitlan.

They are dying of the sickness.

From the Place of the Obsidian-Polishers to the place where grain is threshed, from the precinct of the temple priests to the hovels of the fishermen. A district here, a district there. Reports keep coming in. Three families dead in the neighbourhood that borders on the market-place. Another family in the street where the basket-weavers live. An official of the emperor, who is called the Keeper of the Chalk, has buried two of his wives. Three eagle knights have died. I have not heard of any deaths among the jaguar knights, not yet, or among the higher noblemen, but they are surely not immune.

First here, then there. Then everywhere.

No Moor has fallen ill.

He strikes down whom He strikes down, that fellow in the bathhouse said. It is in the hands of God.

These younger men, these newer men, believe it is a sign.

Then Egypt's dust turned into lice and they covered everything. One louse for every grain of dust. And the pharaoh still refused. Then biting flies filled the air, scrabbling in people's hair and leaving bloody marks upon their skin, daily tormenting them.

Like the insects of the marshes here.

Was it flies or wild beasts?

And then there came a pestilence, but not on people, still not yet. A sickness of the animals that spread from field to field. The horses, mules and camels died. The sheep, goats and cattle died. Their corpses lay upon the earth.

When I think of that I see the wreckage of the caravan.

It keeps coming back to me, as it does, I would suspect, to every Moor in Tenochtitlan. A stark, recurring vision. Somewhere on this continent, in the vastness of the New Maghreb, along the road we all have walked, some once, some many times. In some dry wadi or ravine, or on a slimy riverbank, in a stony desert place or else a forest thick with trees. The bones of baggage animals, the stumps and entrails rife with flies. Sad corpses littered here and there. One, at least, lies headless.

The soot from Egypt's furnaces then drifted out across the land, and on every person's skin it touched there sprouted boils.

On every person's skin it touched. But not the skin of the Israelites.

The boils wept. The people wept.

But not the chosen people.

It is the time of Friday prayers and I sit outside the mosque, thankful of the emptiness and peace about the courtyard. The sky is clear, the pale sun is gleaming off the minaret, and a fat unmoving cloud is heaped upon the mountain. The shoes of the faithful lie outside, some plain, some pointed at the tips, some intricate with gold brocade, some leather, some shod with uli soles. Mohammed Issa's are there, as creased and worn as he is.

Sitting on the fountain's lip, I close my eyes and listen to the imam's voice within. This is the story that he tells.

The story of Egypt's plagues.

But the tale is not the same as the one my father knew. The Torah and the Qur'an are in divergence here. The imam speaks of locust swarms, and lice, and frogs, but also of torrential rains that demolished people's homes. And then the water turned to blood. But the firstborn did not die.

As I sit, my fingers find a broken shape beneath my thigh. It is a fragment of the tile that decorates the fountain. These tiles were fashioned locally, from the red-brown clay of Mexica, unlike the tiles of the mosque that came all the way from Andalus, and they were not fired or glazed so crumble roughly to the touch. My thumb erodes the fragment's edge. Bits of it fall away.

They have five plagues, we have ten. It is a different telling. Even the words of God take different forms in different mouths, are mutable and slippery. This is heretical. I think about my father and the way his stories often changed, merging into other things, like the stories of my wife.

The smoke swirls in the mirror.

Sleep did not come to me last night, or not enough of it, at least. Drinking xocolatl late is not a good idea. I used to take a single morning cup and never more than that, but ever since the news arrived things have been confused. I have taken four or five at intervals throughout the day, relishing their potency. My wife has brought them to me.

The feeling of the tile beneath my fingers brings her form to mind. Warmed by the sun, part smooth, part worn. Her arms. The hollow of her back. Her neck. The strong lines of her thighs. Last night, in nothing but her skin, she crouched to grind the beans. From the divan where I lay I studied every part of her, though the lantern light was dim. I looked for marks, for telltale spots of inflammation. There was not a sign.

Perhaps she is marked with lamb's blood.

The imam's tale does not contain an angel with four thousand wings, but still one hovers over us. It rises over Tenochtitlan like an eagle in hot air. Standing silent in the wind, it plunges earthwards like a stone.

A child here. A woman there.

But not the chosen people.

When the prayers are at an end I stand to watch them spilling out, my countrymen. My fellow Moors. The people of the book. The merchants and the younger men, excitable and chattering. The converts, hushed and stern. Here comes Mohammed Issa. I watch him bending for his shoes, jostled by the other men, and fumbling to put them on. His heels drag as he walks.

Peace be with you, friend, I say, as he approaches.

And with you, he says.

They are the wrong way round, I say.

What?

Your shoes.

Ah, he says. Ah. He stoops to swap them round. He does not make his rasping laugh, the way I thought he might. His manner is most serious.

All is well? I ask him.

He has them on correctly now, the left shoe on his left foot and the right shoe on his right. He does not give an answer. He looks disgruntled and confused. Perhaps I have embarrassed him.

How was the sermon? I enquire.

It was fine, he says. Eli...

Yes? I ask.

Some of the men... the younger men... Well, they are saying things.

What kind of things? I ask.

He sighs and shifts uncomfortably. There is embarrassment on his face.

Things about my wife? I ask.

No, about you, he says. Of course it is ridiculous. Ignorant. A stupid joke. Like something that one tells a child to frighten it at night. I am sorry to tell you this...

Get on with it, I say.

They say the mushrik priests bring you blood, from the temples, he says. In bowls. That you mix it up with maiz. That your wife makes bread with it.

What?

On the Sabbath, he says.

I laugh. I cannot help it.

Issa grins uncomfortably, showing horse-like teeth and gums. So you are not worried, then? he asks.

Let them think that if they like. It is a fairy tale. There are more urgent things deserving of my worry these days. Not least the mushriks falling dead.

Yes, he says. He looks relieved. Eli, I must go, he says. Those merchants, whom you met before, no longer wish to trade with me. The news about the caravan has greatly disconcerted them. They will not sell their skins to me.

Their skins?

Their jaguar skins. I hope to convince them otherwise. We are meeting presently.

Wait, I say.

I cannot, he says. With peace, my friend.

With peace, then.

As he goes I have an image of his wife, the one who died. I do not recall her name, but her face comes to me clearly. Issa was the first of us to take a mushrik for a wife, and she was among the first to accept the strangers' faith, to recognise the only God. I remember Issa's face, proud and strong, on that day. All of us were proud and strong back then, or so it seemed. Perhaps he would have settled there, but our mission called us on, to venture ever further west. After we left Qubah, his Taiyno woman stayed behind.

In his absence, did she keep her faith?

It did not save her.

The sickness now has altered many things in the lands where we have been. I am aware that what I knew back then, in those proud, strong days, is no longer as it was. That nothing is the same. That deserted villages stand along the coasts where men once teemed, their roofs collapsed, overcome by weeds. That nations have emptied out. That fields have turned to forests. That Taiyno refugees have fled across the Qarib Sea to settle on those scattered isles where Moors have not yet visited. That is what the stories say.

What stories will be told about us here, in the years to come?

After the final plague, the fifth or tenth, I do not know which, the pharaoh set God's people free. On that the books agree. They left the pyramids behind and went home to the promised land.

But this city is my home. This is my promised land.

A group of converts passes me, keeping tight within their ranks. Some have faded blue tattoos, some are striped with scars. Their jewellery has been removed from perforated lips and ears, leaving holes that have not healed. They are people full of holes.

They go together through the gate to disperse into the streets, into the sickened city. There seem more of them than before. But I have kept no record. Hasan and his friends watch the little group depart.

He is forever watching.

Bowls of blood. I shake my head. Is he behind that nonsense tale? Nothing is clear to me. The tile fits in my hand. It is a broken triangle, something missing, out of place, a piece to be put back again, and I stoop to find the space it fits, to return it to its place. But I cannot see the shape that makes the pattern whole.

This afternoon the offerings started at the temple.

The first I knew of it was a wisp of greyish smoke rising from above a roof. It was not cooking smoke. It started out weak and thin before ascending eagerly, reaching up towards the sun. I did not mention it. At a certain altitude the smoke was troubled by the wind and dragged untidily south-east, where the smoking mountain lies, like a finger pointing there. White smoke lay on the mountain.

In my mind I could see them merging and mingling, becoming part of the same thing, and the vision troubled me. But the grey was smudged away before it reached the lake. Nothing more came for a time. Perhaps, I thought, a false alarm.

But now there is another plume. It rises thicker, darker.

Still I do not mention it, but others notice soon enough. Heads turn. Fingers point. Someone says a prayer. The younger men gather in the courtyard and around the gate, gossiping excitedly, their voices thrilled and scandalised. Those poor devils, one of them says. But he speaks with relish.

Have they killed those Chichimecs? asks my neighbour who deals in silk, his hand above his eyes to shield his vision from the sun. I do not know why he thinks I know. The assumption bothers me.

Chichimecs burn green, I say. Grey smoke is for Moors.

His eyes bulge. He stares at me with a look of mute astonishment, and several other people turn.

It is just a joke, I say.

Moors, Eli? he says, shocked.

A joke, I say again. Yes, perhaps those Chichimecs.

With a frown he turns away, mouthing words I do not hear.

Everyone burns grey, I say.

But it does not help.

A number of the younger men depart together through the gate, saying that they want to get closer to the spectacle. They will not get far, of course. It is prohibited. The quarter where the temples stand is shielded by high walls, and entry is barred to any Moor unless at the official invitation of the emperor. But there are certain streets that allow for vantage points. These fools will stand there open-mouthed, squinting and giggling, fascinated and appalled, while the priests perform their work, minute, atop the pyramids. The imam strongly disapproves but he cannot stop them.

I watch them go with distaste and yet I feel indulgence too. Was I like them in the early days? Did the blood surge in my veins? The first time I witnessed it, in Moctezuma's company, I felt a thousand miles removed from the ceremony taking place, as if I were looking down the wrong end of a Frankish spyglass. I saw small men far away, having small things done to them. The occasion was a festival but I do not remember which, perhaps the Festival of Rain or the Festival of Maiz. Afterwards I went back to my room, which was poorly furnished then, and lay in bed for several days in a kind of lethargy. My mind was blank and dull. Malinala brought me food and washed my feet and lay with me. We lay together truly then, not like we do these days.

Do your people do such things? I asked. Do they also feed the sun?

The Mexica feed the sun, she said. My people are the food.

By that she meant the Nahua, from whom she was stolen as a girl, and sold, then sold again, but those captives were not Nahua. Neither were they Chichimecs. I do not know what they were. My people are the food, she said. Like maiz.

I have not forgotten that.

I have no people, she has said, however, at other times.

The second time I witnessed it I did not feel bad at all. Instead I noted down the numbers for my chronicles. After that it was routine, part of the pulse of living here, like the feasts, the festivals, the dances and the harvest days, the Passovers I marked alone and the Eids the Muslims shared with me, the caravans passing back and forth, back and forth, the nights, the days. I scratched the numbers in my books along with my accounts of trade, of dirhams gained and dirhams lost, of exchange rates and deficits. This is a habit I have kept up throughout the years. I thought one day to count them up to see how many there have been, how many hearts have been required to keep the sun from going dark.

It blazes whitely in the sky. I also have to shield my eyes.

I do not keep a tally now. The numbers make me weary.

These days there are other numbers that I should be noting down. The figures keep coming in, unverified but credible. A couple here, a handful there. Now the quarter of the silversmiths, now the district that adjoins the shrine to the Dog-Headed God. Reports from trading villages that are scattered around the lake. I cannot see it in the sun, but the Angel of Death hangs over us.

Not over us. Over them.

Over Malinala. Us.

This morning I asked my wife not to walk out in the streets. It is no secret now, I said, everybody speaks of it. The imam yesterday in the mosque...

I do not care what the imam says, she said.

I am concerned for you. So many have been falling ill.

Why should I be safer here? she asked.

I had no answer.

So you want me to stay home, she said. Like any Moorish wife. Like any Mexica wife.

Yes, no, I said, unsure.

My man of dust, my ugly deer, she said. You cannot hold me.

And yet I held her anyway, by the arms and then around her back, clasping her shoulder blades, breathing mouthfuls of her hair, which smelt hot and sweet like grass. She stroked me on the head as one might a child. Issa's wife died of it, I said. His wife and child too. And now the sickness has come here.

Now it is here. Now I am here. Now all of us are here, she said. Then she disengaged my hands and kissed their palms one by one, first the left and then the right. It is in the hands of God, she said. Is that not what some would say?

I had no answer to that either.

But she has stayed home today, despite her remonstrations.

Eli, Abd al-Wahid says, how many? Have you heard a count?

A count of what? I ask, annoyed.

What the priests have done today.

Why are you asking me? I cry. I do not know, for the love of God!

There is no need to shout, the big man says, offended.

I grind my fists into my eyes. I have not been sleeping

well, I say. Talk of death is everywhere. A rotting head sits in my room...

Shh! he says, glancing around, but there is no one standing near. The young men have gone through the gate. The grey smoke still rises. Tomorrow is the day? he says.

I will go to the Black House, yes.

Alone?

As you asked, alone.

Together we watch the smoke.

There are two columns now, side by side, from separate fires. From the Temple of the Sun and the Temple of the Rain. They escalate in tight ascending coils, unbothered by the wind, a spiralling calligraphy. Then the drums start beating far off in the city.

Now it is here. Now I am here. Now all of us are here. Where have I heard those words that Malinala spoke before? Hasan, I think suddenly. When I met him in the marketplace. It is an echo. Thumping drums.

Take that head, says Abd al-Wahid. Present it to the emperor...

But before he can nag me more the thump of drums amplifies, much closer than they were before, not coming from the pyramids. The drums are at the Caliph's Gate. The street erupts in noise. And now there are calls and cries, the ragged thunder of feet, and the Moors who have departed hurry back through the archway, more excited than ever now.

Another Flower War, they shout. More are coming in!

*　　*　　*

I make no attempt to count. It is uncountable. It is a river streaming past, eddying and jostling, floodwater that has burst its banks, bearing human flotsam. This time the knights are intermixed, the eagles and the jaguars, in their feathers and their skins, respectively beaked and fanged in their bedraggled headdresses. The faces of the men inside are grim and battle-weary. Their lines of captives trail behind, not only men but women too, old men, old women, children, women bearing children, children in the arms of men. There seem entire villages. They have not just caught warriors but anyone they could find. Through the dust the whites of eyes, in wonder, flash this way and that, gazing at the tall stone streets, the monumental architecture, for these are folk from far away who never saw such things before, who have only known great Tenochtitlan in stories or in nightmares.

So many, says Abd al-Wahid, standing near me in the crowd. Do you have any idea from where...?

Do not ask me, I say.

Why did no word of this reach us? The scale is immense. Why did no messenger bring news? The warriors must have been abroad for days, scouring the countryside. Why did we not know of this?

Did Malinala know?

City mushriks line the street but none throw flowers today. They only watch, their expressions as weary as the warriors. One onlooker has a face as spotted as a jaguar skin, but it is his own skin, multihued and pustulated. I know him from the marketplace. He used to sell me amaranth. When more captives hurry past I lose sight of him. Women, children, old men, gaping-mouthed and stupefied. They have the look of netted fish dragged out of water. The scalding light. The hard-edged streets. The hostile, blinding element. So many! There must be thousands now. But I have given up counting.

Painted shields, obsidian blades, spears, pennants, feathers, masks, dusty men and dusty women staggering to keep the pace. The human river rushes on. The sight is dizzying. One woman falls and is dragged by the rope that binds her hands, her bare feet kicking in the dust, until the man beside her halts to put her on her feet again, then falls himself, and is dragged kicking in his turn. A child wails. The drummers drum. A feathered man blows a horn. And then a glimpse of something else, a longer, darker face, an orange beard, a turban cloth. It is the rider who was knocked from his horse by a cob of maiz. Wait! I cry, but he is gone, vanished in the multitude.

What, Eli? says Abd al-Wahid.

One of ours, a Moor, I say.

Where?

But now I am not sure. I cannot see him any more, can only see the backs of mushrik heads, departing mushrik backs, no darker skin, no shackled figure tall enough to be a Moor, for surely any Moor would stand much taller in this crowd. And surely any Moor would have the sense to turn and call to us.

Nothing. A mistake, I say.

Eli?

It was nothing, I say.

Are you unwell? asks Abd al-Wahid.

This city is unwell, I say.

It was nothing, I am sure of that, yet still I saw his face. Confused, alarmed, I look for more but can see only mushriks. Mushriks with their smeared skins, their shining hair now dull with dust, hundreds, thousands perhaps. Inside each of them, one heart. Each heart thumping out of time. How many to satisfy the sun?

The drums are growing distant.

The last of them goes past and the street is clear again. Two spectating crowds are left, one mushrik and one Moor. The people of the flaming sun and the people of the crescent moon. They are on the sunny side and we are in the shadow. The Mexica converts shrink away as if exposed suddenly, but it is not they whom the blazing light exposes. Now that the knights have gone, trailing their ropes of hearts, the evidence of sickness in the watching crowd is on display. Faces squint, puffed up with boils. Skins are speckled red. They look as if they have been shot with darts, eaten alive by ants, glowering and shivering. They turn away from us. I feel our separation now as I never did before, the things that make us not the same. It is just as Issa said. We never were the same.

At last the onlookers disperse, but one woman is left behind. Ragged, almost naked, she is squatting on her haunches. It is the mother of the stricken girl from the neighbourhood of ducks. She reaches out her hands to me.

Crossing the vacated street, I make my way towards her.

She is not reaching out to me but to anyone, no one. There are pustules on her fingers. She stares unseeingly from a face that is transformed. She will not last long,

I think, not from what I have seen before. My legs tremble as I crouch.

Lady, it is me, I say, my face level with hers.

Her heavy breath smells like a drain. Lord of strangers... she says.

I have spoken with my God, I say, as you asked me to. The Faceless God. The God of Strangers.

From across the sea, she says.

From across the sea, I say, wishing that I had my handkerchief infused with lemon-scented oil, the oil that drives the flies away. The smell of her is sickening.

But I am marked with lamb's blood.

Your daughter, is she still alive? I say.

The sun is going out, she says.

My God will help her soon, I say.

Lies. I am telling lies. But what else can I do? I glance back at the other Moors, who cannot hear my words. A few of them are watching me, the merchants and the younger men, some curious, some with looks of scorn. The old dhimmi in the street, the fool, with the dying mushrik. It does not matter what they think.

My little girl, the woman says.

The Faceless God spoke to me. I heard His voice, I say. He bade me give you this for her.

My hand is searching in my robe for something, for anything.

The sun is going black, she says.

My God is stronger than the sun.

My fingers close around the broken triangle, the shard of tile. No, I cannot give her that. Where is my amulet?

The charm against the evil eye that I bought from the marketplace, the one my wife would not accept. Beside the rough tile, something smooth...

Ah, here, I say.

I press the thing into her hands. The pretty bead of blue glass with its ring of lighter blue, its pupil as black and bright as a mirror of obsidian.

This will keep her safe, I say. You should hang it around her neck.

She takes it without seeing it, hiding the eye inside her fist.

Now go, I say. Away from here. We cannot help you further.

I do not look back at her as I retreat towards the shade, towards the crescent moon that gleams on the topmost point of the minaret. The only thing I want to do is go home and wash my hands. I step around a guard, two guards, whose hands are on their scimitars, and in my haste almost collide with a group that has been watching me. They are some of the men who left to see the spectacle, but they did not get far. I recognise them. Hasan's friends.

Excuse me, I say, as I attempt to make my way. One fellow does not move aside. There is laughter on his lips. The dhimmi has found another wife! he says. He may soon be needing one.

I take a step without a thought. My fist meets his eye. There is a crunch, a shriek from him, and he falls sprawling in the dirt.

I am Ambassador to the Sun! I roar.

He clutches at his face.

Slight me, but do not slight my wife! She is more than any one of you.

Then I continue walking.

Back in the safety of my rooms I open my fist, which hurts. Inside is the broken tile, snapped into several pieces now, and I wonder if the fellow's face is also broken. A charm against the evil eye. His socket wet beneath my fist. I take the shattered bits of tile and throw them in the corner.

The second time I met him there his face was bruised, his forehead scraped, as if he had been in a fight. The same distrustful, pinched brown eyes, like pools of murky water. It was a quieter time of day and the teahouse was unoccupied. I took the table next to him, though I could have sat anywhere.

Tea, I said to the boy. And then I asked the Christian, Wine?

He did not say anything but I poured it for him anyway, filling his cup furtively from the bottle I had brought. Under the caliph's law alcohol was not allowed, but it was available. I had bought it from some Frankish sailors near the harbour.

This man was a sailor too, people said, a foreigner. He came from the port of Genoa on the Middle Sea. Once he had captained his own ship but now he was just a drunk. He was mad, others said, an infidel and a sinner. I had made enquiries in the alleyways behind the wharves, where gossip flows from every part of Andalus. This man was a laughing stock, I heard. A fantasist. A dreamer.

Something in his manner, though, had made me seek him out again. The wine-stained papers I had glimpsed.

Calculations. Maps and diagrams.

He had spoken of a voyage.

His ramblings made little sense and were tiresome to listen to, a litany of grievances. He was bitter, secretive, angry and resentful. I poured him wine and let him talk in his rough seaman's Arabic, the common tongue of the Middle Sea. I understood it well enough, inflected though it was with peculiar words and phrases. He claimed to have come from Qurtubah, directly from the caliph's court, where he had sought an audience. But his request to speak with the caliph had been denied. Before that, so he claimed again, he had been in Frankish lands, in England, Genoa, Venice, France, seeking audiences there. The kings had only laughed at him.

Cowards. Sons of whores. Damn them. May devils torture them in hell. May they drown in piss, he said.

They laughed at you for what? I asked when the profanities had ceased.

He glared at me suspiciously. I have great plans, he said.

He would not say more that time, just sat there gulping back his wine. Through his fingers I could see words in Arabic, Latin, Greek. His stubby hands lay on his papers like two crouched, defensive crabs, guarding them jealously and yet displaying them to the world, or displaying them partially, or displaying them only to me. Numbers. Lines of latitude. His manner was coarse and hostile, but, in his vanity, he wanted me to look at them. Or that is what I told myself.

He did not say more that time. But I went back every day.

Every day I gleaned a little more from his foul-mouthed diatribes, picked a thread of meaning from his cursing and complaining. This Genoan was a learned man, or at least he had been until rotting his mind with wine, and he spoke of astronomy, geometry, navigation. He had read the works of Greek and Arab philosophers, and knew the circumference of the earth. He had studied how the wind blows west on the Sea of Darkness. Between heaping scorn on the ignorance of Christian kings and the rudeness of the caliph, who would not even meet with him, he spoke of zeniths and degrees and the span of continents. Fifty-six and two thirds miles, he reckoned, equalled one degree. A mere two thousand miles of water lay between Qadis and the Indies. He jabbed at a diagram, mouthing terms I did not understand, and then recoiled suspiciously and glared at me with hatred.

You are like the rest of them, he snarled. A pig. Go to hell.

More wine? I asked. The liquid glugged.

With a scowl he knocked it back.

Why did he confide in me at all? To this day I do not know. Perhaps because I gave him wine. Perhaps because I listened. Perhaps because he recognised something of himself in me, that I was an outsider too, not just a dhimmi but something else, that I wanted greater things from life, adventure, glory, happiness, was not content to be content.

Something of himself in me. Is it still there, I wonder?

*　　*　　*

Why am I thinking of him now, so many years afterwards?

Perhaps, towards the end of things, one thinks about beginnings.

Beginnings. Ends. They are the same, that is what Malinala says. Time is not straight but cyclical, as the world is not flat but round. I have always thought it strange that the Mexica, who do not use wheels, see wheels inside everything, wheels of numbers, stars and time, while Moors see history as a line that goes from one point to the next, from creation to apocalypse, from light to dark, from new to old, from order to entropy.

The world was dark, my wife says. And then came light again.

The Fourth Sun was not he but she, she says. She of the Jade-Green Skirt. Once the wife of the Lord of Rain, now the wife of the Smoking Mirror. She ruled rivers, storms and seas. From between her legs, beneath her skirts, water flowed out constantly, in torrents, never drying up. Within that water children swam as multiple as fishes.

I close my hand into a fist. It hurts. I open it again. It hurts. One of the knuckles is split. The flesh is bruised and red. Perhaps there is a fractured bone.

My warrior, said my wife.

She did not ask what had occurred nor how the injury was received. No doubt she had already heard. She hears everything. From a jar she daubed the skin with a substance made from lakeside herbs, a salve to take the swelling down. There, she said. She kissed my hand.

Then she prepared xocolatl.

She of the Jade-Green Skirt gave life to the world, she says. As women give life to the world while men take it away. But the Smoking Mirror, her husband, who had stolen her from the Lord of Rain, was jealous of the life she gave. He was jealous of her love. The crippled, one-footed god, lord of the night sky and prophecy, of magic and trickery, made her weep with cruel words. He made her weep with insults. He made her weep by saying that the love she gave the world was hate, the life she gave the world was death. The words he told her broke her heart. She wept for fifty years.

I am listening with half an ear, for my mind is on other words. Now it is here. Now I am here. Now all of us are here. Hasan almost said the same when I met him in the marketplace, after I had witnessed him conversing with the messenger. It links them, two links in a chain.

I tense my fist. It throbs and aches.

But she did not weep tears, she says. From her eyes fell blood. The rivers rose and they were red. The lakes and the seas were red. The bloody waters rose and they covered everything. The deserts and the mountaintops, the fields, the cities of men. All men drowned, apart from those who turned themselves into fish. The world was drowned. The sun was drowned, guttering in blood.

And once more it was dark again.

It did not end there, she says.

No more, I say. It is enough. No more stories, no more suns. Tell me what is real for once.

This is real, she says.

Tell me what is going on.

There was one fifth, final sun.

No more! I cry, in fury now. What is happening here? That Hasan with his mocking friends, his top lip shaved bald as a dog's. How dare you all laugh at me?

I am on my feet, staggering. The xocolatl courses through me. I have drunk six cups today, too many, I will never sleep. I try to seize my wife's arm, but my hand hurts too much.

What have you been doing? I shout, not caring who hears me. The Woman of Two Tongues, that is what they call you here...

Before the Fifth Sun dawned, she says.

Shut up!

Before the Fifth Sun dawned, the Feathered Snake and the Dog-Headed God went to the underworld to recover mankind's bones. They gave their blood to make men men.

I do not want to hear it! I will not be made a fool of. Your smoking mirrors everywhere...

Now it is time to give them back. We have been the food, she says.

No more! What is it that you want? Did you kill my water-god?

Malinala laughs.

We eat of the earth, she says.

What?

Then the earth eats us. Quiet, my heart. My warrior.

What are you doing?

Shh, she says.

She takes my injured hand in hers and presses it. I gasp with pain. She brings it to her dry lips and kisses it, once, twice. Then she presses it again. Ah, I say, tears in my eyes. She brings it to her lips again.

But the pain is a good pain.

Then her lips move to my wrist, my arm, my upper arm. I take a handful of her hair. The Woman of the Knots. She bites the soft flesh of my arm.

We have been the food, she says again.

Her hands are in my robe. God, I say. I close my eyes.

But soon, she says, soon, my man of maiz, we will be eating.

· EIGHT ·

WHILE she is on top of me a yellow lizard crawls behind her head, where the ceiling meets the wall. Yellow with black spots, it is stalking some small prey. Then her hair falls over my face, a shining curtain coming down, and I cannot see it any more.

How long now? she asks me.

While she is underneath me I see the glyphs of flowers, rain, vultures, sky, spirit and bone, on an untranslated codex that lies open on my desk. The footprint of the water-god is still faintly visible from where it staggered on the page, the red ink of one pictogram blobbed, as if carelessly scribed. How do these meanings connect? But Malinala's elbow sends the parchment to the floor. Its meaning does not matter now. Not now, as she pulls me in.

Long enough, I say, my mouth against her toes.

The room turns. The whole world turns. The lizard reaches out its tongue and seizes a white butterfly, draws it back inside itself, swallows, gulps, turns to stone. A heavy bowl falls off the desk and rolls across the floor.

When Malinala makes a noise I do not care if my neighbours hear, my countrymen who laugh at me, they do not matter any more. Her teeth are on my earlobe. The stars and planets wheel. She has unleashed her hair, has freed it from its binding plaits, and it spills across my desk, on the divan, on the floor, off the bed, against the wall, as we make our pilgrimage around the places of this room, transforming each place as we go. Her tongue is in my ear. The Thirteen Heavens stand above and the Nine Hells lie below. She is She of the Jade-Green Skirt and I am the Feathered Serpent.

How long? I ask now but she does not answer me. Her mouth is open, her eyes closed, like the Flayed One with two skins as he walked by the canal, but the skin is all her skin, hers and no one else's. It is miraculous to me, the feel of it beneath my thumb. I run my fingers over her from the ankles to the hips. Our bodies turn like a wheel and again she is on top, again I am gazing up. The lizard has now vanished. Ah, I say, for my back is bent at a painful degree, and my wife adjusts her weight. Old man, she says and laughs. I laugh as well, despite the pain, and once more I am proud and strong. As I once was. As we once were. This is the finest hour.

This is the finest hour but we have known this hour before, we have lived it many times. Time is not straight but cyclical. The stars go round and round. I close my eyes and we are lying on the dappled forest floor on the march to Mexica, my countrymen not far away, dirt and leaves stuck in our hair, clumsy in our urgency. I urge her to be quiet, my palm against her lips. We are in the place of reeds with the hot sun blazing over us, the reeds thrashing in the light, casting stripes upon our skin. A biting fly nips at my arm. She swats it. I bleed. We are in the place of willow trees, in the blue dawn light, before the sun has met the lake. We are in wet pastureland with horses grazing near us. And now we are above the town in which she served the Mayayans, the town in which she was a slave, with the cool mist on our skins and the uli trees surrounding us weeping out their thin white sap, flowing into wooden bowls. Take me with you, she said then.

I took her. She took me.

Each of us takes the other now. We are breathless in the taking. Her nails leave red marks on my skin, glyphs that are untranslatable. The codices lie on the floor, but we have made new meanings. Man and woman. Dust and maiz. We are the symbols of ourselves, locked into one pictogram. Our teeth bump as we kiss. She playfully tweaks my beard. Her tongue is pink. I taste her sweat. She tweaks the greying hair upon my chest, which was black before. The sun and moon wheel over us. An insect scuttles down the wall. We are two things and yet one, one thing and yet two. The Lord of Duality and the Lady of Duality, in the place where all things meet. She is the Goddess of Bright Sweat and I am the Lord of the Root.

It does not matter any more who hears us, or if my hair is grey. It does not matter that Benmessaoud has sacked the caravan. It does not even matter that, on the shelf that holds my precious things, the head sits rotting quietly in the iron chest where the papers are, the papers that no one has seen, that no one will ever see, its eyelids closed, its mouth downturned, awaiting hell or paradise. All that matters is my golden wife, unpeeled like a maiz husk, below me and on top of me, this moment, now, this finest hour. As she once was. As we once were.

Long enough? she says at last.

I have no breath for a response. The sun goes down, the moon comes up, the mountain vents its smoke. Consuming, I am all consumed. After the ascent, the fall.

A hairless dog howls once outside.

Everything melts away.

We are lying on the bed, which has partially collapsed. I must have been asleep, for the candle flame is low. Beyond the window it is night. A single star hangs in the sky. There is no sound of hairless dogs.

The sky has a reddish glow.

My wife has lit a tubaq pipe, from a store I did not know she had. She is lying next to me, her head upon my arm. Noticing I am awake, she puts the pipe's stem to my mouth, and I inhale carefully.

My head whirls, but I do not cough. The smoke climbs to the ceiling.

Watching it as it rolls to where the ceiling meets the wall, where the lizard caught its butterfly, my mind turns to that other smoke. One column rising straight and true, one madly spiralling. There is no more sound of drums so perhaps the priests have tired, for their work is strenuous. I do not want to think. I take the pipe, breathe in again, breathe out, and it is now I cough, convulsing spasmodically as water floods my eyes. Malinala strokes my hair.

I fall asleep again.

The sky still glows when I awake, a strangely elongated dawn. Malinala is still sleeping. I pull the blankets over us and run my fingers down her back, where the bright sweat has dried, rekindling the miracle, and that is when I feel it. A small, raised point. A tiny bump. The skin around it burning. My fingertip searches for more, but there are none. Not yet.

I do not want to wake her, so I take my hand away.

In the morning she is gone. I had hoped that she would not be.

Everything in the room has been put back in its place. The codex sits on the desk in its correct position. The clothing strewn across the floor has been tidied away, fresh garments have been left for me, my shoes are placed beside the bed. Everything is as it was. There is not a trace of last night's disarrangement.

I hoped that she would not be gone, that she would still be lying here. With her heavy eyelids closed, her hair pooled around her. I would have liked this to be so, if only for a little time, before the day becomes itself. But she is gone. The day is here.

It is 11 Deer, 1 Snake. The day I meet Moctezuma.

My bare feet fumble for my shoes, left into left, right into right. Poor old Issa, I think. I would like to talk with him. For once my bones do not complain as I stand, which pleases me. It is as if they have been oiled. Last night has made me younger. The xocolatl has been ground and the drinking bowl awaits, but that can wait. I can wait. I should make preparations.

Above the embers of the fire hangs a water-filled bowl, into which I pour imported soap that smells of roses. I cup my hands in the bowl and throw the water on my face and watch the noisy drops fall back. With a pair of scissors I tidy up my beard. My reflection watches me from the mirror by the bowl, no disc of black obsidian but a sheet of silvered glass, a mirror not for the night but for the day. There is no smoke to smudge the view. My image flashes sharp and clear. My wet cheeks, my dripping beard, my bright eyes looking back at me.

Lord of strangers, the woman said.

May the evil eye not find her.

I drag a stiff brush through my beard, untangling its kinks and curls, and apply sweet-scented oil. I trim my fingernails. From the pile where Malinala laid them out before she left I select clean underclothes, a long shirt, cotton trousers and a freshly laundered robe. Black. I have always dressed in black. I comb my tangled hair. I adjust the skullcap on my head, the shield between myself and God.

That bump. That blemish on her back. Did I imagine it?

Breakfast has been set for me on the table by the wall. Cactus-fruit, some dates and wrinkled figs, a lump of maiz-cake. I take my meal standing up, wandering around the room, dreamily stunned from last night. Fragmented images. Her fingernails. Her ankle in my hand. The glyphs of grass and rain. Staring at a cactus-fruit I find myself once again gloriously, unexpectedly aroused. Ha! I laugh aloud, spraying out bits of date. Great happiness swells inside, yet at the same time, somehow, I am thinking of the punch I threw, my fist connecting with that mocking eye, the crunch of bone on bone. My hand no longer hurts today. It is swollen but it does not hurt. What happens when I see those men again?

There may be trouble.

There may be trouble, but I do not mind. My heart is full of joy. My wife is once again my wife.

And then I feel that bump again.

In the hollow of her back, that spot. That burning blemish.

Perhaps it was something else, a pimple, something negligible, a mark left by a biting fly. The flies are pestilent this year, that is what Issa said. Not all change is bad, that is what he also said.

But his Taiyno wife. His child.

My appetite has vanished, and I put aside the dates.

It is too much, I cannot think of more than each small task ahead. I stoop to agitate the fire. I spoon the xocolatl. The bubbles rattle in the pan. The steam curls up. I scald my lips. I drink the liquid hurriedly, hardly tasting it. Seized by that energising draft I make my way towards the door, and as I do I see the final thing my wife has left for me.

Two circles, one black, one white. My code to Moctezuma.

My walnut backgammon board, inlaid with ebony and bone, has been placed beside the door, with those two pieces set on top. A token of our amity. We have played together for years. I taught the emperor long ago, and, with his discerning mind, strategic and mathematical, he quickly learned to play it well. This is not a day for games, but it has become our custom. As I feel the weight of it, the varnished wood from Andalus, I remember, with distaste, the other thing that I must take. It is up there on the shelf beside my Torah, my Qu'ran, my menorah, my Qarib shell, in the iron chest with the papers.

The key clicks in the lock and I lift the lid. For a moment I think it will be gone. I hope it will be gone. But no, it is my wife that is gone, while this foul thing is not. I hold my breath against its smell and stuff it into my bag.

I close the lid of the chest and then open it again. Again I reach inside. The topmost papers have been stained by brownish juices from the stump. The cramped, untidy words and charts are smudged, almost illegible. There is no need to read them now, nor at any other time, but I do not want to leave them here. They no longer feel safe.

I slip the papers in beside the head. My bag hangs heavy.

It is long past dawn, but the sky is stained with red. No one seems to be about. The courtyard is deserted. Cautiously I look this way and that, expecting Hasan's friends, or half expecting them at least, but not expecting what I see. The quality of light is strange. A sunken, sullen gloom. A haze hangs over everything, which at first I assume must be smoke from the temple pyres, but the impression is dispersed, generalised, like mist.

Where has everybody gone? I cross the yard towards the mosque. Its crescent moon does not gleam atop the minaret. The silhouette stands flat against the air, sharp-tipped and leaden grey, and as I watch a piece of it detaches and falls away, soars above the rooftops and passes through the Caliph's Gate. A songbird, of a type the mushriks like to shoot with slings.

Many birds have settled on the rooftops, and on the mosque, and on the courtyard's cobblestones. A cloud of panicked wings beats as I cross the courtyard. Some are songbirds, some are fowl and some are even birds of prey, flocked together unnaturally. In the sky swarm multitudes, speckled in the gloom.

There comes a muted roar from somewhere far away, and at the same time the chatter of Moorish voices. As if in a slow dream I make my way across the yard and through the door and up the stairs that leads to the upper chamber with the latticed windows. A crowd of backs is packed in there, all angled away from me, and someone has removed the patterned wooden pane from its frame to allow an unimpeded view towards the east. I strain to see over the heads of my assembled countrymen, although by now I have guessed, I know what they are looking at.

The weeping warrior has wept.

It runs in gouts of crimson.

A twisting column of white cloud is pouring up into the sky, engorged and grossly spiralling, spewing out red sparks. Its colour and viscosity resemble melting fat. Its flanks are scored by vivid streaks, and as we watch another bright stream oozes out and spills towards the mountain's base, negotiating clumsily the rocky contours of the slopes, until its progress is arrested by some natural obstacle and the flow comes to a halt. But only for a moment. There comes another sullen roar and more white vapour is exhaled. A red trace, like a missile, ascends and falls towards the earth, a fiery burning angel. But we cannot see its wings.

Framed as it is within the window, boxed inside its square of sky and lake, hazed by the smoky cloud, the vision is contained. It is happening far away, too far, for now, to touch us. It is like a pictogram, a glyph inked in the codices, which might be read as death or life, the end or the beginning of things, depending on the other symbols with which it might be paired. In this moment, as I watch, it is untranslatable. What its meaning is to Moors, to Mexica, to Tenochtitlan, is not possible to infer. But if I stand here long enough some fool will surely ask me.

Voices rise and fall but nothing is being said. With my heavy bag I turn to leave. Nobody sees me.

The confused, exhausted birds have resettled on the roofs. The anger of the smoking mountain has disturbed the valley. Flocked around the Caliph's Gate, which, as before, appears unmanned, they stir again at my approach and hurl themselves into the air, clattering and clamouring, causing me to shield my face. But it is not my coming that has alarmed them. Hooves are thundering through the gate, a turbanned head ducks through the arch, and through the ashy, sunken light two horses and two riders come. One horse is chestnut, one is roan.

What news? I cry.

The weary men swing from their saddles and drop lightly to the ground. Their horses' coats are scummed with foam, their manes askew and dripping. The riders squint at me from faces that are streaked with grime. One bows to me. The other spits.

Where is the Chief Vizier? asks the man who bowed.

Engaged, I say. Do you bring news?

Water, says the spitter.

Come with me, I say. Did you find the caravan?

Water first, the first man says. We have ridden through the night and did not stop at the lake.

Why not?

In the name of God! the spitter snarls. We are thirsty!

Making soothing motions with my hands, I cross the courtyard to my door. The two men follow me and their horses follow them. I fill two glasses from the cool stone jar we keep beside the door and the riders empty them. Then I fill them again and they empty them again.

Now, I say, after both have slaked their thirst and are refreshed. Why are there just two of you?

We were attacked, says the first.

By Benmessaoud?

Not Benmessaoud.

But you found the caravan?

We found no caravan. Let us tell it piece by piece. All hell has broken loose out there.

We should report to Abd al-Wahid, the spitter says angrily.

Abd al-Wahid is busy, I say. He is watching the emanation. You can first report to me and then to the Chief Vizier.

I would like to drink some smoke, the spitter says.

By the time I have found the pipe my wife has stashed away, and her store of cured leaves, the riders are squatting on the floor, chewing dried fruit from their rations. They look at me with red-rimmed eyes, as weary as the birds. From the way the spitting man takes the pipe stem, greedily, and the way his eyelids flutter as he draws the smoke inside, and the satiated sigh he gives as he breathes it out, I can tell that he is one of those who needs the smoke like food, who hungers after it as Christians hunger after wine. Observing him, I think of the crumbled leaves inside the cotton bag, the handful of dark beans, the things that Benmessaoud, in his piety, would destroy. Has destroyed. Ah, the spitter sighs.

Now, I say. God willing, I shall hear your story.

So, the first man says, after he has drunk smoke as well, though his greed for it is not so urgent as his friend's. So, we went across the pass and took the road towards the coast. We did not ride along the road but through the hills above it. Mushriks were on that road, some going east, some coming west, but we could not tell why. They were not warriors. Then we saw the fire on the mountain and we heard its noise. Red sparks sailed over us. Ahmed's horse took fright at that.

Ahmed?

The third of us. His horse almost threw him off and bolted but we calmed her. Then there was more smoke and noise. Mushriks from the villages were fleeing to the north. The countryside is in disarray, hordes of them are on the move. We continued going east until we reached Tlaxcala.

Benmessaoud is there, says the spitter, thumbing leaves into the bowl of the pipe, not meeting my eyes. He is camped beyond its walls.

You saw him?

Of course we did not. But we saw his banner.

We kept far away and watched from the rocky ground above, the first man says. We counted tents and horses. A thousand, maybe more. There was no sign of the caravan. Its wreckage must lie further east.

Prisoners?

None that we could see. We stayed there for the afternoon, the night. In the morning we were seen. A patrol of horsemen spotted us, but before they could climb the slope we were away. We knew the ground and they did not. They did not pursue us far. Once we had evaded them we considered going south to circle back towards the road, but there were mushriks everywhere. Nahuas, God only knows what else. They were in great excitement. We attempted going north but the slopes were too severe. Steep wadis, cactus thickets, snow. So we turned our steeds around and rode back west again.

He puts an ember to the bowl and sucks. His grimy face glows red, his teeth red, his eyeballs red. As he exhales I detect a smell beneath the pungent smoke, something familiar, putrid, sweet. It is coming from my bag.

Yes, what then? I ask.

Before we reached the Moor's First Sigh we were attacked. A company of eagle knights was descending from the pass and we rode straight into them. Two of them grabbed my horse and I struck out with my sword. I cut one in the neck.

I killed one, says the spitter.

Ahmed's grey mare bolted, says the first man. He was clinging on but the beast had an arrow in her side, I think more than one. Praise be to God the two of us broke through and rode towards the pass. We have hardly stopped since. Once we were well clear of them we searched around the barren ridges, calling out Ahmed's name. But we found no sign of him.

They have taken him, the spitter says. The sons of dogs will eat his heart.

They do not eat hearts, I almost say, but now is not the time. You are sure they were eagle knights? is what I say instead. Perhaps, in the confusion, you...

They were wearing fucking feathers!

Very well. What then? I ask.

Nothing then. We could not find Ahmed. He is dead, or worse than dead. There was foul smoke everywhere, spewed out by the mountain. We almost had to fight our way back across the floating road because of the mushriks there, covered in spots and sores, all of them leaving Tenochtitlan.

Good riddance, the spitter says. It is as Hasan says, that God Himself has struck them down. If they will not accept the faith...

What has Hasan to do with this? I ask, wrinkling my nose. The smell is growing more pronounced.

Who are we fighting anyway? the spitting man cries suddenly. Is Benmessaoud not a Moor, a Muslim, the same as us? Did he not save the caliphate?

He will take that leaf away from you, I say, nodding to the pipe.

The fellow scowls but does not say more. He fills himself with smoke again.

You are very tired, I say. Make your report to Abd al-Wahid. Then you must eat, bathe, sleep. You must tend your horses.

And then? the first man asks. His voice is like a candle flame, guttering, almost out of wax.

And then, I say, all will be well. Come now. Up with you.

The two men take their leave of me, bow-legged, stiff-limbed from the ride, and lead their sweating steeds away as birds shriek in the sky above. I pick up the heavy bag with its stinking cargo. I feel almost as tired as them, but my task is still to come.

All will be well, I said.

But all will not be well.

The words that the rotting head has stained are the same words that I saw the penultimate time I met with him. The last time in the teahouse. He showed them to me readily for I had won his trust by then, or at least had lessened his suspicion. I had worked on him for weeks, sitting patiently through his tirades, letting him explode and fume and douse himself with wine again, wine that I bought day after day, though I could scarce afford to eat. I let the burning secret that smouldered in his bitter heart, the secret of his hatred for the world, and of his hope, reveal itself spark after spark, one glowing ember at a time. I fanned it with my silences, stoked it with judicious praise. The secret of his great, mad scheme.

Instructions for a journey.

See, he said, thrusting the papers before my eyes, see what the cretins do not see. Those bastard kings. Your stupid caliph. See what fate they have refused.

The Latin words of the title page were rendered into Arabic. I began to read aloud.

Shh! he hissed, misting me in particles of spit and wine. In your head, you stupid Jew!

I read it in my head.

A Full Account and Explanation of My
Proposal to Seek a Western Sea Passage to the
Lands of the Indies Over the Atlantic Sea.
By Cristoforo Colombo, a Native of Genoa.

This would have changed the world, he said, but for their deaf ears and blind eyes. I have been laughed from court to court, insulted and ignored. My brothers have derided me. I have been reduced to this, forced to come crawling like a beggar to the infidels, to an enemy of Christ, beseeching him to hear me out. And they shut the door on me! Those pigs. They would not even look...

The sulky lines upon his face warned me that collapse was near, that he was about to plunge into abject wallowing, that tears of pity would flow and glasses would be broken. This state, from what I had observed, was not a useful one. I arrested his descent.

I believe in you, I said, realising as I spoke the words that they were true, that I did. For suddenly across the years I saw, as I had as a boy, that burning sunset at World's End, the golden pathway striking west across the darkness of the sea, an arrow showing me the way. The west wind in my father's hair. His tales of magic islands. Ever since that vision I had known. I had always known.

All I need is ships, Colombo said. And men and money.

There was fire in his eyes, not yet extinguished by his tears.

I can help with that, I said.

Do you have ships? Do you have men?

No, I said. But I have words.

Words? The devil take your words!

The devil will take my words, I said. The devil or the caliph. Listen to what I have to say. Hear me, as they did not hear you. I am of the caliphate. I know the workings of this land. I am not a Muslim, it is true, but a person of the book, a dhimmi, a protected one. Under the caliph's law that gives me standing here. I shall go to Qurtubah to speak with him on your behalf. I speak proper Arabic, not your seaman's brogue. I know the language that he speaks. My father was a merchant who traded throughout Andalus. I am a merchant's son. I will make the caliph hear.

The Genoan did not say anything. His eyes narrowed. He pursed his lips. He shook his head scornfully.

But he was listening.

It was true I was a merchant's son, but I did not tell him more than that. I did not tell him why I was waiting here in Qadis. My father, bless his memory, had died and left money to me, by no means a fortune but a respectable amount. If I had carried on like him, contained, content to be content, continuing the trade in wool from north to south, from south to north, as he had done, as his father had done, as his father's father had done, I would have been prosperous enough. But I wanted happiness. I had invested everything in a shipment from the east, fine goods from distant India which would bring me wealth and fame.

Every last dirham spent. My ship had not come in.

Three months I had been in Qadis, waiting for a sign. Every day I paced the docks, asked questions in the alleyways, scanned the blue, indifferent horizon for a sail. There were rumours of a storm, of pirates in the Middle Sea, but they were only seaman's tales, not to be credited. Every night I walked back from the harbour through the cobbled streets to sleep upon a narrow cot in a room of other men, mostly dhimmis like myself, penurious or destitute. I had almost given up hope.

Those papers were my hope.

Let me go to him, I said. With your plans. Let me talk.

Why should I trust you? he asked, fixing me through his drunkenness with a look of black malevolence.

Because I am like you, I said.

You are not like me, he said.

I will be your mouth, I said.

His purple lips gleamed wetly as he drained his final glass. I do not like you, Jew, he said. And I am not fooled that you like me. I do not seek a friend in this.

I do not ask to be your friend. Only your ambassador.

He stared at me for a long while, his face as blank as the sea. Come to my rooms tonight, he said. We will discuss this further.

Across the green-flecked paving stones, past the broken fountain with the fragment missing from its tiles, beneath the archway, through the gate, I leave the quarter quietly, not troubling to look back. Birds muddle in the sky like smoke. The light is thick and grainy. Down a broad east-facing street there oozes a molten glow, not the mountain but the sun, which has not risen above the roofs of the cluttered buildings yet and throbs deep red, diffuse inside the cloaking haze that mutes the lines of everything. It flashes once, a wink of fire, then it is lost in darkness.

An old woman near me gives a cry that sounds a bit like laughter, or she might be singing. It disturbs me that I cannot tell. She points towards the vanished sun and cries again, or laughs again. I hurry past her. The Black House awaits. The city is unchanged yet changed and small sights keep confounding me, things that are the same yet not the same. There are holes in what I know, pieces that have gone missing. The man I buy kasava from, in his usual alcove by the road, sits pointlessly beside a tray that does not have kasava on. The man who trades in caged songbirds is gone, but not his cages. As I pass the Street of Grains the bent-backed women are absent from their mealing stones, the grinders of blue and yellow maiz, and it shocks me not to see them there unceasingly grinding away, a sound I hear day after day. Instead there is another sound. The mountain's faint, abyssal roar, an indigestive grumbling, with the pulse of drums behind. Sweat has bubbled on my brow. My bag, with its ripened load, swings at every step.

Netted silver fish, half-dead, flop faintly next to the canal, with no one waiting anywhere to sell them or to buy them. From the dimness of a shop where an artisan once worked masks of jade gleam pallidly, with green protruding eyeballs. A group of ragged worshippers is huddling around a shrine to a god I do not know, a god of little consequence in the manifold family of gods but of consequence to them, presumably, at this hour, and among the devotees is a figure I recognise, he of the red and grey painted face, he of the shredded lobes, the Flayed One in his borrowed human hide. His mouth is open. He is dancing in the throng, the sleeve-like flaps of cured skin wagging loosely from his wrists like the tongues of hairless dogs, back and forth, back and forth. He needs no one to guide him now, for his eyes are bulging wide. Blood drips from his fingertips from some flagellation of the flesh, some expiation to the sun. Then the wall of bodies closes around him and he is gone.

Mushriks are leaving Tenochtitlan, that is what the riders said. They are fleeing down the floating road from the city. Where do they intend to go? They will not go south, for the smoking mountain is enraged and the villages are emptying, the countryside is on the move. Will they go east towards Tlaxcala, only to meet with Benmessaoud coming the other way? A thousand horses, maybe more, by the riders' reckoning. Maybe less, but even less would be enough, more than enough, with the city in this state.

Enough for what, exactly?

I do not want to see these things, whatever things are now to come. I am too old for war, for grand eventful changes. Too old for the world to end and too old for a new one to begin. But not too old to love my wife. God! It rushes back.

That blood-warm memory of the flesh. Last night I was young again. The ardour swells inside my skin and my body rages. But then it crumbles, falls to ash, and I stagger on my feet as I feel, once again, that spot beneath my fingertip, as I see, most lucidly, Malinala's strong and beautiful face pox-ravaged and transformed. Her lips made foul by weeping sores. The vision is appalling. Where have you gone? I shout, startled by my own voice, and as I do I turn a corner and there is Coyotl.

He is strolling near some trees, taking bites from some red fruit. He sees me as I see him. He stops. Good sun, I say. But he spins upon his heels and quickly goes the other way, never once looking back. I change my path to follow. He turns into an alleyway and by the time I reach that place he is turning down another. Wait, I want to talk to you! I call. He just walks faster. When I reach the corner I see him far ahead of me, smaller than he was before. Still he has not looked back. Stop! I shout.

He runs.

Last night I was young again, and again I will be young. My uli soles pound the road. I leap some fallen brick-work. The heavy bag swings at my side, back and forth, encumbering me, but I cast all thought of it aside, and of what it contains, and concentrate on my feet, the fleeing messenger ahead. I am gaining on him.

He vanishes down another street but I quickly reach that place and he turns another way. I can catch him, he is mine. What is he mixed up in? I know he has some part in this, this man whose job it is to run, this man who carries messages from mouth to mouth, from ear to ear. I will find out what he knows. I will unpick the pattern. Now I am keeping pace with him, fairly flying down the road, my bag swinging back and forth, back and forth, back and forth, between steep walls and across open ground and down squalid lanes. My breath heaves raggedly. Coyotl springs like a deer, nimbly bouncing on his toes. My crashing footsteps echo off the walls. He flows like liquid. I blunder onwards, gasping now, each step more clumsy than the last, into a small public square. There is a stabbing in my side like a knife going in. Ah. Ah. He flies ahead as if he were leaping mountain ranges. Doubled over in the square, my mouth floods with the taste of bile. When I raise my eyes again, the messenger is gone.

Agonised, no longer young, it takes me time to breathe again. What was I thinking? The stabbing pain has less-ened, but blood is thumping in my ears. The ground swims horribly. At least the square is empty and there is no one here to witness me as I hobble back, knowing I will not catch him now. Something squelches underfoot. I lift my shoe. A mess of pulp, the red fruit that he dropped.

Then I see the shape ahead. The square is not quite empty.

Somebody is lying there, with their head in the sun. Two, no, three, hairless dogs are standing at their side. A woman asleep. Not asleep.

One of the yellow animals stretches, scratches at its ear. Another yawns and shows its gums.

Not a woman. A girl.

Regarding me with depthless eyes, the hairless dogs prepare for me. One grins. Another growls. One has something hanging from its mouth that is not its tongue, something that is dark and drips. Away with you! I shout. I flap my arms as I advance, revolted by the sight of them. Agh! I yell, waving my bag. Their lips curl into snarls. Their bald heads low, they rush at me, snapping and slavering, one on each side of me and the third one at my heels, causing me to wheel around. The bag arcs in my hands. It strikes the third dog on the snout and as the creature leaps away I wield the bag like a flail, lashing out and battering, hearing my trousers tear as one attacks me from behind, feeling the fabric rip, now kicking one in the ribs and then another on the rump, shrieking as if possessed by djinns. Teeth and foam fly everywhere. A furious sundering of my robe. The head! I drag it from the bag and hurl it like a missile, hitting the blue dog in the face and causing it to yelp. It does not yelp like a dog but like a man, a brother of man, a child of the

Dog-Headed God who went into the underworld. Take it if you must! I cry, thinking that the brutes will pick the head up by its ears or beard and scamper off with it. But, to my surprise, they scamper off without. Across the trampled square they run, their naked tails between their legs, turning once to look at me.

Agh! I scream again.

Panting and perspiring, I stoop to gather up my things. My bag lies savaged in the dust. There is froth upon my robe. My clothes are ripped. Sweat blinds my eyes. One of my shoes has fallen off. The head has rolled across the dirt, face downwards, and I turn it round to see that it is scuffed and soiled.

I am sorry, brother, I say, returning it to the bag.

Not wanting to, having wiped the filth and spittle from my clothes, wanting only to walk away but knowing that I cannot, I approach the sleeping girl. Of course she is not sleeping. Her clothes and skin are torn away where the hairless dogs have worried her, but I recognise her face despite the disfiguring boils. She looks peaceful and confused. Black ants are crawling over her. The charm against the evil eye dangles from a knotted cord. I am sorry, I say again. I leave the charm for someone else to find and go on my way.

And what is there left to say about this walk through Tenochtitlan? Only that dogs are everywhere and that the sun is dark. Only that I hardly glance at the temples when I pass them by, for there are no crowds gathered there, no costumes or festivities, no vendors selling yellow peppers, nuts, spit-roasted water-gods, honeyed sweets, fried grass-hoppers, popped maiz, cakes or cactus wine. Only that the smoky sky is teeming with frightened birds, that the temple steps are wet, that body after body rolls down the angled, steep decline, their torsos blue, not green but blue, that the priests are distant dots that lift and bend, lift and bend, exhaustedly carrying out the work that has no beginning and no end. That the drums have lost their rhythm and have become one thunder. That the rider Ahmed's heart might be among that multitude, if it is not already smoke, and that there is no one who would know, no one who would care, not even me, especially me, for it is not my business now. Past the gardens by the lake I approach Moctezuma's palace.

Many knights stand at the gate, fanged and feathered, bearing clubs, and officials of the emperor with elaborate hats and headpieces whom I barely notice as I show the Moorish Quarter's seal, the crescent moon inside the flaming sun, and the sigil of my house, the menorah with the initials E.B.A., which is my name. I pass untroubled through their ranks. Lush gardens lie beyond. There is the menagerie with cages containing jaguars, bears, wolves, lizards, snakes, exotic beasts from distant lands, the pool containing crocodiles, the aviary of bright-plumed birds, but I have seen enough of savage creatures for one day. Through a statued courtyard I pass slaves tending flowers. At first I think they are watering them, but no, they are wiping off the ashes that have settled there, on the petals and the leaves, dabbing them clean with cloths. But more keep drifting down. At the top of a flight of steps there is a tall, narrow door with a costumed knight on either side, one eagle and one jaguar. Grimly they watch me come.

Peace be upon you, I say. Good sun. Let me in.

Identically they stand aside. Petals are scattered in the hall. I leave the searing light of day. The door to the Black House opens.

· NINE ·

TWENTY-NINE years ago I walked through another door, leaving the light of day behind and passing into shadow. My shoes did not tap on stone but whispered on soft carpeting, my ears were not filled with drums but with gently lilting music. No mushrik knights stood at that door but a pair of silk-swaddled Moors with ornamental halberds crossed to bar the way that lay ahead. An announcer spoke my purpose and the halberds were uncrossed. Before me stretched a forest.

It was not a forest of trees but stone, a thousand columns holding up the weight of a granite roof that soared high above my head. Inlaid with marble, onyx, jasper, porphyry, white and black and red, the symmetry flowed as I walked, identically repeating. Vertical stone trunks and arches, vertical stone trunks and arches, ranged as far as I could see. The Great Palace of Qurtubah. Ever since I was a child I had heard legends of that place, but never, in my strangest dreams, had I thought that I might enter it.

Never, in my strangest dreams, had I thought a lot of things.

Your Eminence, your Highness...

The words ran through my head.

Since leaving Qadis I had journeyed for two weeks down dusty roads, past villages, through olive groves, over mountains and hot plains. I had slept in caravanserais, in peasants' fields, in ditches. My money was gone, spent on Frankish wine that I had not drunk, on food that I had barely touched, but chiefly spent to buy me time and company, to buy me trust. The trust of a distrustful man.

It had been a good investment.

The papers were in my bag, sewn into the lining in case I were attacked by thieves, but several times on that long walk I had unpicked the stitches. I had sat by sunlight and by starlight, jealously glancing around in the way that he had glanced, protecting them as he had done, committing to my heart the words, the calculations. As I walked I rehearsed for the audience to come, in rhythm with my trudging feet. Your Eminence, your Highness, Mighty Caliph, Sword of Andalus...

The columns came to an end. Small red lanterns hung from chains. There was a sweet, rose-petal smell. Ahead was a golden glow.

He sat upon a cushion with a vizier on each side of him. I kept my eyes upon the floor as I had been instructed. Conscious of my unwashed clothes, my Jewishness, my lowly trade, I bowed my head and waited there with my hands behind my back. The papers rustled in my hands. My hands were trembling. A vizier bade me speak, but when I tried the words would not come out, and when I cleared my throat it sounded coarse and insolent, and so the first word I uttered was an apology. He wafted an indulgent hand. I felt his slow eyes watching me. The vizier prompted me again, and now the words came clear.

Your Eminence, your Highness, Mighty Caliph, Sword of Andalus, Shield of the Faith, Commander of the Faithful, I come here as your servant.

He gave a brief, impatient sigh. What is your proposition?

Cautiously I raised my eyes. I saw a fat man with a beard.

I come to you most humbly, I said, to offer you these plans. For an expedition westwards to enrich the caliphate.

I took my hands from behind my back and held out the papers. The caliph did not look at them. He only looked at me. I did not move, just waited there, caught in the silence between worlds, not knowing what my fate would be, between one lifetime and the next.

The great man shrugged and scratched himself. Go on, he said at last.

Twenty-four thin triangles, twelve ebony, twelve ivory, with the pieces, black and white, placed in their twos and threes and fives. Click. I set one black one down. Click click. He sets two white. Neither of us says a word as we prepare the backgammon board, each taking care to line the pieces up just so where they belong, the way I taught him years ago, the way my father once taught me. Click click click. It is routine.

Is it strange to feel at home here?

The room in which we sit is black from ceiling to floor, with four black walls and two black doors, one of which I entered by. It is black but black has many shades, blackness is not uniform, and the muted lantern-light reveals dim figures on the walls, black on black, the shadowed forms of the painted gods surrounding us. The Left-Handed Hummingbird, the Feathered Snake, the Lord of Rain, She of the Jade-Green Skirt, the Smoking Mirror and a host of lesser, smaller deities, each petrified in their pose. No daylight penetrates. On one side of the dais on which we sit is a brazier, tinkling with orange coals. On the other side, upright, stands a great obsidian mirror.

Moctezuma, the Frowning Lord, Emperor of the Mexica, sets his last white piece in place. Noticing one misaligned, he adjusts it with his finger. I drop the two small dice into their cup and rattle it.

The dice jump across the board. One six and one four.

I move my first piece to the left, click click click click click click, and again, click click click click, to make my stack of five a six. The emperor shakes the cup.

The dice jump. Two twos. Doubles.

Moctezuma does not wear his feathered cloak, his weighty torcs, his great unwieldy headdress that sways almost as tall as him. The jade adornments in his nose and lower lip are absent. There are no pearls around his neck, nor at his ankles nor his wrists, no gilded sandals on his feet, and neither is his body pierced, as it is on certain days, with slender needles from the rite of letting blood to please the gods. His fingers are free from jewelled rings and ornaments. Certainly the lantern-light does not gleam on powdered gold that burnishes his skin, as when we first met. He is plainly garbed today. For an emperor, anyway. He wears a simple gown trimmed with small red triangles, an ayate scarf around his neck. His head is bare. His feet are bare.

There is something changed in him.

He is not called the Frowning Lord because he is inclined to frown, or at least he does not frown more than others I can think of. His eyes, I have always thought, are kind, creased with the wrinkles of his smiles rather than his scowls, heavy-lidded, sharp and bright. His lips are delicate. His nose is narrow and refined, with nostrils that are rather wide.

I know these features as I know the arrangement of this city.

There is something changed in him but I cannot say exactly what. His face is the same face, laid out as it always was. But his mouth is pinched and strained, there is a dullness to his eyes and muscles twitch in his jaw. Old. The emperor looks old.

No, it is more than that.

I shake the cup and roll the dice.

Click click click. Click click.

I have always played with black, as he has always played with white. Black for the darkness of the moon, white for the blazing sun. The emperor has the kind of mind that views the world symbolically, that attaches meaning, sometimes subtle, sometimes plain, to everything. It was he that chose these colours when I first explained the game. In the years that we have played, he has often spoken of the other meanings that he sees, the triangles, dark and light, like pyramids, for night and day, the pieces for the peoples of the world, for Mexica and Moors, or Mexica and Chichimecs, or even Mexica and gods, and the hopping journeys that they take, determined by the random dice, from left to right, and right to left, or east to west, and west to east, in the direction of the sun or counter-sunwise, as a symbol for the way that all of us must walk the earth. From one position to the next. Now in company, now alone. Until our journeys are at an end.

Until we reach our home.

The conversations we have had, as these pieces migrate around the board, have ranged through time and politics, history, philosophy, alchemy, God, the gods, life and death. I have spoken to him of things I would never discuss with Moors. Black and white, for moon and sun, we have forged our friendship in this game.

But today the emperor does not speak. The pieces click in silence.

He shakes the cup, spills out the dice. One one, one three. He makes his moves. His white piece lands on one of mine and sends it back to the start. Its journey must begin again.

I gather up the dice.

There is something missing here, something that is misaligned, but I cannot think exactly what. And then I see it. Normally there are three of us sitting close around this board, for Malinala is always here, between us, her eyes on the game. She does not play, of course, and seldom does she speak, and when she does it is only to translate from one tongue to the next, from Arabic to Nahuatl, Nahuatl to Arabic. The third link in the chain. Even after I had learned the language of the Mexica, and could speak as well as anyone, we kept this custom when we met. Malinala was my mouth.

She was his mouth as well.

You should leave your wife at home, is what Abd al-Wahid said. I have done just as he asked.

I wonder why the Frowning Lord has not commented on her absence.

But then the Frowning Lord has not commented on anything, not even when he greeted me. His customary loquacity has given way to silence. Once or twice his mouth has moved as if he were about to speak, and once or twice his eyes have shifted nervously, regarding me, or glancing past me at the shadowed corners of this shadowed room. Is he watching something there? The idols of his gods? There is something furtive, almost timorous, about the man, whose fluid nobility has always been so effortless, whose every gesture, in the past, has been artful and composed. Not well. He must not be well.

Dice tumble from the cup.

The coals shift in the brazier and a flare of flame licks up, yellow on the walls, and dies. The walls sink into black again.

Click click click. Click click click.

Not illness. Something else.

As we play my nose detects, once more, the sickly, cloying smell from the object in my bag. This stupid plan of

Abd al-Wahid's. What is it meant to prove? It reeks, but incense has been scattered on the orange glowing coals, a fragrant resin sourced from pine, whose sweetness mingles with the stench. The emperor has not noticed it, lost in his private silence. The recollection of the head reminds me of the great events unfolding now beyond this room, outside the black box we are in, more fateful and more complicated than this game of black and white, where everything is in its place. I should break this silence now.

But I find myself afraid.

The Black House is not the emperor's court, nor his room of state, nor the place in which he receives his noble visitors, his advisors or his priests, ambassadors from distant lands, supplicants, petitioners, messengers or chiefs of war. It is where he comes alone to meditate and to pray. I have never asked him why he chooses to play backgammon here, to meet with Malinala and myself, to share cactus wine, but I am honoured by the fact. This is his private sanctum. No other Moor, as far as I am aware, has been invited here, not the Chief Vizier, nor any other merchant from within the council or without. My presence here is testament to the emperor's regard for me. To the friendship that we have. Now I must use that friendship.

My lord, I say eventually.

The emperor does not seem to hear.

My friend, I say.

The emperor faintly nods.

I have spoken in Arabic, for he understands some words, but I switch to Nahuatl for what else must be said.

No need for Malinala here. I have my own voice now. I wonder briefly where she is, though something in me seems to know, a revelation I suppress even as it comes to me.

The burning spot upon her back.

I cannot think of it.

Some said there could not be peace, I say, setting down my words as carefully as the pieces on the board, each one in its place. Some said there could not be peace between our peoples. Both Moor and Mexica said this. That we were too far apart. That our ways were not the same. But when I came to Tenochtitlan I saw an affinity.

Despite the many things that were terrible and strange to me, and the many that were marvellous, I found things I recognised. Commerce. Trade routes, merchandise. Markets boasting goods as rich as any in Andalus. In the stories of your people, I heard stories of my own. Your eagle and our burning bush. Signs from God. The chosen people. We have both walked through a wilderness to find our promised land.

I have been happy here, I say. There has been peace between us. We came in peace, and you have given us peace. Friendship. Amity. A home, though we are far from home.

He sighs and stacks his pieces.

I have never wanted more than this, I say, taking up the cup. I have never wanted more than peace between our cultures. The crescent moon inside the flaming sun. Our little quarter here. You with many gods, us with one. This has been possible. But when we sailed across the sea, when we proved such things could be done, we opened up a door. I opened up a door. Now, others have stepped through. Surely you have heard of this?

He blinks and sighs.

They are not like us. They do not want peace as we do.

As I speak I shake the cup, roll the dice and make my moves. Two of my black pieces now have reached the board's third quadrant. The emperor shakes, rolls and moves, click click click, click click click click, and one white sun is almost home.

His eyes are dull, unfocused.

An army comes to Mexica, I say. A thousand horses. Men who are trained in war, who come here to make war on you, who will destroy all we have done. They say that God has sent them here. Now they have reached Tlaxcala. The Tlaxcalans will not fight them, for Tlaxcalans are your enemies. They will help them on their way. They might even march with them. Soon they will reach the Moor's First Sigh, and then they will reach the lake. They will fall on Tenochtitlan as they fell on our caravan. Surely the news of that reached you?

Your move now, he mumbles.

His fingers push the cup to me. They are trembling.

This is serious, I say. My lord, what action will you take?

Play, he says in a kind of moan. He cannot bear to look at me.

My friend...

Peace! Moctezuma cries in Arabic.

In all the years we have been friends I have never heard him shout, have seldom heard him raise his voice. His always was a quiet strength. His power was his stillness. That word, or its opposite, echoes flatly off the walls, or off the mirror's glassy sheen, like the ripples of disturbance on the surface of the lake, like the smoking mountain's voice erupting in the quiet air, and what I feel inside is dread.

Play, he says again.

One of his pieces is exposed and I had hoped to capture it, but the dice do not favour me. Instead I make a stack of five blacks in the third quadrant. He takes his turn, covers his exposed piece with another white, and with the second dice he sends his first piece to the end.

Home. He removes it from the board and makes no comment.

You bid me peace, I say, not caring if I anger him. But tomorrow will not bring you peace, it will bring disorder. Your knights are chasing after hearts, emptying the countryside, instead of readying for war. They must defend the city. They must sink the floating roads so this army cannot cross, they must shut the gates to them.

My knights will do as they must, the emperor says vaguely.

This will be no Flower War, I say, no symbolic dance. These new Moors will not respect your customs and traditions. These men fight for conquest, for purity, in the name of God. This is what they will do...

My hands are delving in the bag.

This, look...

They fumble over something slippery, seize some hair. He has sent us this, I say.

By its beard I haul it out, undignified, puffed and blue. One sheet of the Genoan's papers is gummed against its cheek. I pull the paper off and crumple it back with the rest, redundant relics as they are, and let the head hang in the air.

Moctezuma stares.

You think your city is strong, I say, but your people are dying in the streets. The smoking mountain is aflame. Have you not seen the signs?

Moctezuma frowns, attesting to his moniker. Maybe Abd al-Wahid is right, this is the shock he needs.

The head rotates from side to side. The emperor narrows his eyes.

A yellow flame jumps up again.

Then Moctezuma laughs.

His laugh is not a normal laugh, it is high-pitched, cracked and strange. His shoulders shake as if a private earthquake is in motion. He puts his palms up to his face, and when he brings them down again there is water in his eyes.

My city is not strong, he says. My city is rotten.

Slowly I put down the head, between us, proximal to the board. Sad and foolish, there it sits.

Moctezuma laughs again. He blinks. Two long tears spill.

The head stares blindly at the game as if appraising the next move. But there are no other moves. The emperor clears the board. With a motion of his hand he sweeps the pieces to the floor, scattering the blacks and whites.

No more games, he says.

I wait, not knowing what else to do. The emperor dabs his eyes. The tears have made bright lines down his cheeks, which are pocked with scars from ritual bleedings through the years. I know the history of his face, its hollows, ridges, marks and lines, as well as I know anything. I have seen him shed more blood than tears.

Two spills of water. That is all.

The dice, I notice pointlessly, have landed on two sixes.

You speak of signs, he says. Yes, I have seen the signs. Come. You will see them too.

I hesitate when he stands.

Come, he says again. It is over. Do not be afraid.

He extends his hand to me. I stand.

Where are we going? I ask.

Far. Not far, he says.

With his fingers on my arm he guides me across the room, away from the burning brazier. We cross the blackness of the floor, scattered with fallen pieces. The basalt hardness underneath my soles gives way to something soft, and I glance down at the interlocking geometric pattern of a carpet on the floor, hexagons and octagons and multi-pointed stars, their colours muted in the dark. It is the gift we brought here from the caliph long ago. At the centre of the carpet's symmetry, upright, the mirror stands, the same height as a man. A great disc of obsidian, darkly lucent, blackly bright, convex and smoothly circular.

The emperor stops before it.

Everything is here, he says.

My lord? I ask, confused.

227

Look, he says. What do you see?

I look into the polished stone. Nothing, I say.

In the beginning was nothing, he says. His voice is flat, unlike the gently bulging stone, which bends the light and our reflections looking out. From nothing came everything, he says. To nothing it will return.

My lord, there is not time for this...

You are right, there is not time. Everything is at an end.

He puts his arm around my shoulder, and, within the inky pool, his reflection does the same, seeping with liquid symmetry. He nods. His reflection nods. In planes of black our negatives gaze back at us, black Eli and black Moctezuma, a dhimmi and an emperor, old men, one bearded and one not, old friends, unlikely as that seems, but one of them full of dread and the other, it seems, deranged. For the emperor must be mad. That laugh. Those spilling tears. If I cannot make him understand then everything will be lost, this peace, this city that is my home. But the black mirror holds me.

It holds me and I cannot speak, cannot think what words to say, can only look into the blackness as the black-ness looks at me. The emperor's reflection speaks.

Tell me what you have heard, he says, of the Fifth Sun.

The Fifth Sun? I repeat, as the black Eli repeats.

You surely know the tale, he says. Tell it to me now. You will tell me its beginning and I will tell you how it ends.

If you wish me to, I say.

I rub my brow, and the black Eli rubs his brow. I take a breath. He takes a breath.

I think of Malinala.

The Fourth Sun had ended and the world was drowned in blood, I say. Some of the men were fish but most of them were not. The Feathered Snake and the Dog-Headed God went into the underworld to recover mankind's bones. They mixed the bones with blood and maiz and shaped it into men. Men walked the earth but everything was dark, there was no light. So the gods built a fire to make another sun.

The emperor is listening, his black, reflected eyelids closed, gently nodding in the stone. For now I will humour him. He is not himself, he is not who he was. This is not a time for tales.

The fire burned bright, I say. It burned, and when it was most hot the gods asked for an offering, another god, to step inside and be the Fifth Sun. A strong god called the Proud One stepped towards the flames. But the heat was too intense. He flinched. He could not step inside. He tried again and flinched again. The gods called him a coward. And then a weak and humble god, whose body was covered with sores, whom they called the Pimpled One, ran up and leapt into the fire. Filled with shame and jealousy, the Proud One followed him.

So two suns rose above the world, two suns at the same time. This could not be, so the gods threw a rabbit in the Proud One's face, to mock him and to dim his light. So he became the moon. The moon chased the Fifth Sun across the sky, jealous of his brightness, and the chase goes on today, the moon following the sun, through the years, through night and day. But he is not fast enough...

Blood, says Moctezuma. His eyes are open wide and his charcoal image watches me, blinking in the polished stone. Blood, he says again. That is why the moon cannot catch the sun, because the sun eats the blood and the hearts of men, who must give themselves to him. They eat his light, which gives them life, and in turn they must be eaten. That is why my knights must fight the Flower War, why my priests must labour on the temple steps. To move the sun across the sky. To keep the sun from going black. As emperor, I have done my best. But now the sun is ending.

Something seems to alter in the black mirror as I watch. The clarity of our reflections dims, distorts and mingles. A haziness swirls in the stone, deep within its ink-black depths, smudging what is on the surface, blurring clear lines like smoke.

I close my eyes and open them. The smoke recedes, redoubles.

The chase is ending now, he says. The moon will catch the sun. I have seen what is to come. I have seen the signs. The sickness of the strangers spreading throughout Mexica, my people dying in the streets. The smoking mountain venting flame and the sky going dark. The lake will rise, the water will turn red, the gardens will be drowned. There will be biting flies. There will be lamenting. I have seen the men of whom you speak, the men of purity, riding on their swift deer, in their hundreds, in their thousands, pouring from the east. They are like a river.

Where have you seen them? In this polished rock? I ask.

Through her I have seen, he says. And more will follow after. They are the people of the moon, and, jealous, they will catch the sun, they will drag it from the sky, for the sun is weak and sick and all our blood is not enough, all our hearts are not enough, they have never been enough. The demons of the moon will devour us. She has told me this.

Who has told you this? I ask.

The Fifth Sun is coming to an end, he says. The sky is dark.

Who is she? Whom do you mean?

But the emperor is fading. His laugh is gone, his frown is gone, and he is collapsing now, folding in on himself like something that a fire has burned the substance of and turned to ash, crumpling and crumbling, diminishing as I watch. He does not scour the world with wind or flames, does not weep tears of blood, does not summon jaguars. He just gets smaller. I watch his figure shrinking in the blackness of the smoke that seeps and scrolls beneath the stone, obfuscating everything, and in that cloudy nothingness I see, or I think I see, or I cannot be sure I do not see, the tumbling forms of men and horses, flames, buildings rolling down, like glyphs that have come alive, that stretch and merge, bursting their bounds. I try to hold him on his feet. You must be strong! I say.

But something else stirs in the stone, darkly distant, in its depths. Something black, shaped like a man, swiftly drawing nearer.

It is not too late, I say.

The figure flows through the dark towards us, gathering density. It grows and thickens as I watch.

They are already here, he whispers.

I do not turn around. The black shape looms behind me. Its smoky lines have coalesced, solidified, into certain form. Man-shaped. Woman-shaped.

Moctezuma bends his knees and descends to the floor. His reflection disappears, but there are still two reflections. Black lips, black eyes, knotted hair. Even now I do not turn.

Caught in the silence between worlds. Just for a moment longer.

Her reflection looks at me and my reflection looks at her. Reversed, negated, still we wait.

Good sun, I say at last.

I turn around. Her face is bright. Her dress glows white against the dark.

Peace, my heart, she says.

She pours the steaming xocolatl into a drinking bowl and places it in my hands. I breathe it in. So rich, so strong, my body sweetly trembles. Nobody can prepare this drink of gods as can my wife, even now. Especially now.

Here at the end of things.

The dark aroma fills the room, that sumptuous expanding cloud, covering the sweet smell of the incense and the rotten smell of flesh. My wife has picked the scattered pieces, suns and moons, from off the floor, has put the useless dice away, has cleared the backgammon board. She has fed the brazier.

She has covered up the head.

Moctezuma is still sitting on the carpet on the floor, underneath the smoking mirror, regarding her incuriously.

He is there and not there, an absence in an emperor's shape, or a piece of architecture that has served its use. Already a forgotten glyph, a symbol without meaning. He has not said anything and nor have I, not for some time. I have merely watched as Malinala has prepared the pan, as she has so many times before, clinging, for a moment more, to this small ritual that we have, this rite of domesticity, numbly waiting for its end.

It is almost a relief.

Now the bowl is in my hands, the thick black fragrance fills my nose, and Malinala takes a seat where the emperor sat before. The drinking bowl is made of gold. It was made for royal lips.

I take a sip. It scalds my tongue.

Drink, says Malinala.

I swallow, take another sip. My nerves fizz. My body sighs. My injured hand, which has not hurt all day, is aching sorely now, cupping the heavy golden weight.

How long? I ask. How long have you been coming here?

I know the answer she will give.

Long enough, she says.

Have you... have you been with him? I ask, stumbling on my words, but even as I form the thought I know that it has missed the mark.

What do you think? asks my wife.

I slowly shake my head.

Then what is it you have done? I ask instead.

She glances at the emperor coolly and appraisingly. I have told him stories, she says.

There is no guilt in her. She sits calmly, straight, unmoved, her hands crossed neatly in her lap. She is serene and innocent. At peace. No marks or blemishes.

There are no sores upon her face. No sign, yet, of the sickness.

And Hasan? I ask, taking a deeper drink. Last night, I thought...

He is nobody. An emissary, a go-between.

An emissary to whom? I ask, but even as I speak I know the answer to that too.

Malinala moves her eyes. And then the black door opens.

A man steps into the room. Well-composed and lean. He has a neatly trimmed black beard and robes of charcoal grey. His head is shaved close to his skull. His right hand rests upon his chest. He nods to her, then nods to me. Peace be with you, he says.

And with you, I say, as he walks across the room. His footsteps hardly make a sound. He does not greet the emperor nor acknowledge his presence in any way. His every movement is precise. He squats between me and my wife, keeping his feet flat on the floor, as one would when on the road to avoid the muddying of clothes, or when one is not stopping long. The posture of a commoner. His gaze is mild and direct.

In a quiet voice he says, I know who you are.

Smaller than you would think, said the man I once met in Yuqqatan. Like someone you would pass on the street and not recall his face.

I know who you are too, I say.

His manner almost like a clerk.

Eli Ben Abram, he says.

Benmessaoud, I say.

Malinala watches me but I do not look at her. In my ears, now close, now distant, throbs a rushing roar. It is like waves crashing up against the walls of a cave, or like the sound that can be heard by pressing a shell up to one's ear, my conch shell from the Qarib Sea, to hear the white surf echoing. A ragged, rhythmic thundering. Does it come from the mountain, the blood-soaked temples or my veins?

The mild man shifts on his haunches, holds me in his steady gaze.

God willing, he says, I shall be Emir Benmessaoud.

I drain the last drop from the bowl and set it down upon the floor. It makes a heavy golden clunk. My veins, the sound is in my veins.

Emir of what? I ask.

Of Mexica, he says.

I take a lungful of air and slowly let it out again. I feel the xocolatl surging on the wave of breath. I listen to my heart, here at the end of things.

My soldiers are at the pass, he says. They shall be here in one day, two days at the most, God willing. My cavalry could be here tonight but the Tlaxcalans slow them down.

Tlaxcalans?

Them and Nahuas. Malinala's people.

It sounds wrong, my wife's name in his mouth. It is not his to utter. But then neither is it mine. Not any more. It never was.

Why? I ask in Nahuatl.

But I cannot look at her.

My wife speaks in a gentle voice. Revenge, she says simply. On the ones who eat my people. On the ones who sold me. Ever since I was a girl I have dreamed of this.

I glance again at Moctezuma, who has closed his eyes and is gently rocking back and forth, lost in soundless conversation with his gods, or with himself. There is nothing left of him.

You have used me, I say.

You have used me, she says.

I put my hands over my face and breathe. Warm wind against my palms. I have only ever wanted peace, I say in Arabic.

Benmessaoud nods thoughtfully. I too want peace, he says. My soldiers are not murderers, not savages. They are men of God.

How many Muslims did they kill when they destroyed the caravan?

Benmessaoud looks at Malinala and then back at me. Your caravan is safe, he says. You can thank your wife for that. By now it will be at the coast, and soon the things it carries will be on their way to Andalus to corrupt the honest Muslims there, and onwards to the Frankish lands, to the markets of the infidels. That filthy drink, the leaf that smokes, those idols of abhorrent djinns, all the other filth you have been sending across the sea. But that shipment is the last. Your mushrik trade is over.

But... but what of that? I cry, pointing wildly at the head. Who is he, in the name of God?

The roar in my ears gets louder.

One of mine, says Benmessaoud, glancing at it casually. One of my men of God, who was not so godly. He raped a woman on the coast, a mushrik, and planned to marry her. He received his punishment. And now he has done his duty.

You sent it as a sign, I say, to make us think... Who brought it here?

That man who runs, says Benmessaoud. The messenger Coyotl. He has been reliable.

And Hasan? What is he?

A go-between, as Malinala said. He came ahead of me. Him and some of the other men who fought with me in Andalus, who see this empire, and the caliphate, for what they truly are. Ungodly. Rotten, like that sinner's head. Things to be cast away. He has prepared the ground for me, as Malinala has prepared the emperor for what is to come, for what is unavoidable, for what cannot be undone. She delayed your meeting here until I reached the city. Now you know enough of me, and will know the rest in time. But I know something of you too. Something that the caliph does not.

His tone is cordial. He leans forward with his slender arms across his knees, his soles still flat upon the floor, relaxed and conversational.

There are rumours, he says, of a teahouse in Qadis.

Malinala watches me. I can feel her eyes upon my face.

They say there was a foreigner, a Genoan, who talked incautiously. A Jew was sometimes seen with him. The Genoan disappeared. Soon afterwards, a Jew went to the caliph to reveal certain plans that had been revealed to him, so people said, as if by the voice of God.

I will not look at her. Her body in the dark last night. The heat of her. The cool of her. That bump beneath my fingertip. Does she know that it is there?

The mild man says softly, There were rumours of a body.

I briefly close my eyes, my own black room in this black room. What is it that you want? I ask.

Peace, like you, he says. There could be a place for you in building this new empire, my Emirate of Mexica, a country that is strong and pure. Abd al-Wahid, that indulgent man, is one of those I do not need, but your skills could be useful here. There will be no Moorish Quarter. The whole city will be for Moors, and the Mexica that stay can have a quarter of their own. They must submit to God, of course, but that process has begun. Hasan has been busy here.

And what of me?

The caliph's law is done with in this city. You can submit as well or you can leave, it is your choice.

I glance towards the Frowning Lord, or the shape that he once occupied. He is an outline on the air, like the paintings of his gods.

And him?

Benmessaoud looks bored. He is also done, he says. After he has stepped aside he will stay here under guard, in this black room. He will not be harmed. He can live his days out here, in blackness, with that mirror.

By his eyes you would know, I say. That is what he said.

Blandly and inquisitively, Benmessaoud regards me.

A man I met in Yuqqatan, who told me he had fought with you. By his eyes, he said, you would know that he is blessed.

And what do you think, murderer? Tell me, thief. Am I blessed?

I look into his eyes but only see myself in there. When he blinks, I disappear.

We are both blessed, I say.

Then I stand, pick up my bag and make my way towards the door. Benmessaoud does not rise nor make a move to stop me. My ugly deer, says Malinala as I pass her by, but I cannot look at her.

Stay, she says as I reach the door.

Come with me, I say.

There is nowhere else to go. A new sun is coming. Stay.

Let it come. You will die here. The sickness is everywhere.

Then I will die everywhere. Stay. You are my man of maiz.

No. Good sun, my heart. I am dust, I say.

I do not walk back through the streets but along the eastern shore, where the floating gardens are. The gardens have been trampled. The stalks are battered down. Reaching out, I tear a yellow cob from its husk of leaves, draw back my arm and fling it hard to watch it turning in the air, end over end, above the lake. It meets the surface with no splash. No ripples spread from it. The sky above the lake is grey, streaked with red, engorged with ash, and the smoking mountain is a silhouette inside the gloom, an emblematic triangle, unreal and faintly grumbling. The warrior is weeping flame. His tears are flowing crimson. The exhausted sun has all but disappeared, swallowed in the smoke, now dimly pushing its way through then stuttering and faltering, leaving just a shadow of itself, a fading memory. Flocks wheel in the air in patterns of confusion. The floating road across the lake is thronged with ambulatory crowds, barging and bustling, heading to the furthest shore, and overladen kanoas are teeming on the water. The floating maiz cob dips and rocks, is overcome by lapping waves, and is gently lost from sight. I watch until it is gone then hurry onwards.

At the place of willow trees, from where I watched the caravan depart a few short weeks ago, although it feels like months ago, from where the riders rode away a few short days ago, although it feels like weeks ago, I enter the city by the Gate of the Left-Handed Hummingbird. His visage grimaces, the god of war and the sun, but he cannot lead his people now. A helpless, ugly child. The crowd of mushriks jostling confusedly through the gate do not even look at him in their clamour to vacate, and neither do they look at me. Their eyes are full of sickness. Baskets of vegetables and brimming gourds and sacks of grain are in their arms, upon their shoulders, children are slung around their backs, ducks and huehxolotl-birds and other fowl dragged behind on ropes or in cages made of sticks, hastily convened possessions carried on a sprawling tide. Where are you going? I want to ask. There is nowhere else to go. That is what Malinala said, the Woman of Two Tongues,

Three Tongues, but her words mean nothing now. How long has it gone on for? How many years has she been visiting the emperor, her words like swirling smoke inside the black stone of his heart? How many months has she conspired with Benmessaoud? Coyotl has been running back and forth with their messages, between this city and the coast, Hasan and the younger men have been working quietly, a convert here, a convert there, and our eyes have been blind. My eyes have been blind. Back there I could not look at her and now I cannot think of her, neither of what she has done nor what will be done to her, the mark of death upon her back which, by now, might have spread to her shoulders, belly, thighs, invisible beneath her gown, and soon will reach her breasts, her throat, her face, her lips, her eyes. It is a sign from God, that is what some might say. But that God is not my God, as the idol on the gate is not the god, not any more, of the men and women in the street with weeping babies on their backs, with their chattels in their arms, fleeing from the sickness already inside them. Where can they go? To the mountain's fire, to the steel of Benmessaoud? One day, two days, God willing, that is what that mild man said, and I could give them warning now, could tell them what is on its way, but why, here at the end of things, would they listen to my words? I am Eli Ben Abram, I am Ambassador to the Sun, but my name means nothing now and the sun is ending.

What do you think, murderer? Tell me, thief. His eyes like stone. Against the swelling crowd I push, going northwards through the streets. I must salvage what I can, the codices, my chronicles, the few small treasures that I own, before I join this exodus. For this is not my home now. This is not my promised land. Past the Street of the Artisans, the Square of the Sharpeners of Knives, a ransacked shop, a broken spear, I find the shrine to the Dog-Headed God garlanded with bodies. At first I think that they are children, naked, pink and flayed, but no, they are hairless dogs, spreadeagled, with their skins peeled back. The sight revolts me more, somehow, than the action at the temples. A singing crone shuffles past, tapping on a little drum. Devotees of the Feathered Snake are dancing in an alley. Pyres of sticks are smouldering, sticks or bones, in pyramids, throwing their smoke into the air. There are ashes in my beard, ashes on my eyelids. Through the Caliph's Gate I go, past the twisted olive tree, no birds, not even butterflies, but shoes are piled near the mosque. Passing, I peer into it and see the imam's finger raised, pointing up to heaven. I cannot see Hasan's face but I know that he is there, as he has always been there, as he has been everywhere. What happened to that votive knot of hair beneath the carpet? Blood-drinker! someone shouts, one of Hasan's acolytes, not the man whose face I cracked but one of his companions. I have no time to waste on him and so I go quickly on. Where is Abd al-Wahid? Where is my friend Issa?

My door, which is not marked with lamb's blood, has been rudely pulled aside. As I step into the room I half expect to see her. Standing with her back to me, in white, with lilies in her hands, her hair unbound, bright and black. Come with me, I will say. Or naked as she was last night, her body unmarked by signs. A new sun is coming. Stay. But there is nobody here. The place is in confusion. As I look across the wreckage of what used to be my room, once again I am not here but in a different quarter. The dirty garret where he stayed in Qadis, its walls hung with maps, bottles strewn across the floor. He had been drinking heavily. This is where I found him. After we had set our terms we spat upon our palms and shook. I will be your mouth, I said, I will make the caliph listen. But as I turned away to leave he tried to grab the papers back. I have changed my mind, he said, I do not trust you. I tried to reassure him and to remonstrate, I did my best, but the man assailed me with his fists and with his feet, shouting, spitting, lashing out as if he were devil-filled. He pulled the papers one way and I pulled them the other. They will be ruined! I yelled. But he was beyond all sense, and I struck out with my fist and when he fell I continued hitting him until he stopped. My hands were pressing at his throat. His cheeks were turning blue. His greasy locks were curled about his ears, his sightless eyeballs bulged, and I knew that even if some passer-by had heard the noise it was unlikely they would come. He was a man alone, unloved, and would be forgotten. I smoothed out the crumpled papers and folded them carefully, as they are still folded now. My feet crunched on broken things. I left the wreckage of the room...

My feet crunch on broken things. My desk is overturned. Ink is spilled across the floor, my favourite drinking bowl lies shattered, and the precious codices have been torn and trampled on, their bindings ripped, their pages slashed, some splashed with ink, some partly burned. Fragments of my chronicles lie similarly despoiled. Half a cactus on a rock, black footprints scrawled across the earth, half an eagle, jaguar teeth, a blade of grass, a flaming sun, scraps of glyphs lie everywhere, their sequences and meanings lost, not to be deciphered now. The stories are destroyed. My holy books and my menorah have been removed from the high shelf and the iron chest is open. But the papers are in my bag.

Leaving this mess behind I cross the courtyard, thick with smoke, past the mosque from which both Moors and Mexica are spilling out, past men with panic in their eyes. Dual explosions echo from the smoking mountain. A woman screams beyond the wall. O my children! she cries. Into the stables I go, the stalls with their sweet smell of hay. Most of them are empty but for rats and rotten grain. The chestnut and the roan are here, not quite recovered from their ride, and the roan still wears her saddle as the groom has run away, the riders are nowhere to be seen, so the roan is the one I take. She stamps and shivers nervously. I mount, not well. It has been a long time since I rode swift deer but the knowledge is in my thighs, my calves, my cracking knees. I dig my heels into her sides and exit at a canter. Her hooves ring on the cobblestones. There he goes! someone cries. White-robed bodies rush at me, hands reach out to grab the reins, someone drags at my bag. With a kick I send him sprawling. Let it all come down on you! I yell as my horse rears above the crowd, as my heels gouge, as together we break through the throng and fly towards the gate. A stone thumps me on the back, but I am not pursued. Once beyond the Caliph's Gate I rein my steed for one look back. Abd al-Wahid's gleaming face is framed in a high window. He is in the latticed room, alone, so far as I can tell, perhaps barricaded in, and is gazing down on me distantly and mournfully, like a picture from a memory. I raise a hand as I depart, but he does not move a muscle.

The hooves beat on the stone-paved streets, the dusty central thoroughfare, beneath the Gate of the South, through the place of willow trees, and thunder on the floating road, across the shining, swarming lake, towards the dim and distant shore. My passing leaves a startled wake through the evacuating crowds. In the middle of the lake I thrust my hand into my bag, pull out Colombo's papers and fling them upon the waves, not glancing back to see them fall. His words can feed the water-gods on their final voyage. The floating road comes to an end and the hoofbeats drum on mud, through yellow grasses, over stones, through the scattered camps of refugees that sprawl along the shore, upwards now, along the winding road the caravan once took, into the purple hills that rise towards the mountains. Maiz fields and cactus slopes, pastures where our sheep once grazed, the roofs of distant villages, abandoned shrines beside the road. At a remembered vantage point I turn. The city floats below in the black mirror of the lake. The pyramids. The broad canals. Like something from a marvellous dream. Then the ashen cloud rolls over and Tenochtitlan is gone.

*L*izards scuttle on the rocks, delving into shaded cracks.
Flowers that I cannot name seethe in the hot wind.

Pairs of eagles trace slow circles in the cloudless sky above, casting shadows on the soil that flow, distorted, into rifts and fissures, over fractured earth.

Lines of ants go back and forth, bearing looted treasures.

I have ridden for three days to reach this barren countryside. This place of stones. This place of thorns. This place that is far from cities. I have not been this way before and I do not know the road ahead.

The road behind is dark and veiled. There is no going back.

At last the hills come to an end and the land is flat below. A shining river wanders like a thread of burning metal. There are no trees. There is no shade. The horizon is a yellow blur, uncertain, hazed into the sky.

It looks like a place of death. But beyond it might be wonders.

I have ridden for three days since turning from the Moor's First Sigh, which for me was the last. I did not pause there long. I saw them there, the men of God, with their banners fluttering, the sunlight dazzling on their steel, descending from the rocky pass into the green valley below. Brightly clad Tlaxcalans and Nahuas marched behind. We have been the food, she said.

Smoke bloated up into the sky. The clouds were red with the mountain's flame.

But soon we will be eating.

There was no one else to witness it. I watched and then turned away.

The land around me looks like clay that has been shattered by the heat. Everything is smashed and loose and nothing holds together. Brittle rocks break apart beneath my stolen horse's hooves as we go down, through groves of thorny cactuses, to lower ground.

There are snakes and spiders here.

It crawls with biting flies.

The sun, in its final appetite, blazes white and terrible. Its fiery road across the sky collapses into blood. Rabbit-faced, the sallow moon weakly chases after it, round and round, in starry wheels of time.

There is no going back. The stories are all ended now.

But before me lies a continent. This boundless New Maghreb.

Beyond this burning land, perhaps, is a place of green grass.

I put my heels to my horse's sides and continue my descent.

GLOSSARY

This novel retains the original Arabic names for the cities now known as Spanish. Indigenous American words that entered English via Spanish remain in their original Nahuatl or Taíno forms (the languages, respectively, spoken by the people living in the Valley of Mexico and in many of the Caribbean islands, including Cuba).

Italicised words and names are my own inventions.

dhimmi	'protected person', a non-Muslim in a Muslim state
Frank	generic term for European, Christian
Gharnatah	Granada
huehxolotl	turkey
huracan	hurricane
Ishbiliyya	Seville
kanoa	canoe
kasava	cassava/manioc
Qadis	Cadiz
Qarib Sea	Caribbean
Qubah	Cuba
Qurtubah	Cordoba
maiz	maize
Makkah	Mecca

Mayayan	Mayan
Middle Sea	Mediterranean Sea
mushrik	polytheist
New Maghreb	literally 'New West'
Old Maghreb	'Old West', i.e. Morocco and North Africa
Sea of Darkness	Atlantic Ocean
Taiyno	Taíno
tlilxochitl	vanilla
tomatl	tomato
tubaq	tobacco
Tulaytulah	Toledo
uli	rubber (from Nahuatl olli)
water-god	axolotl, also known as the Mexican walking fish
World's End	Cape Finisterre
xocolatl	chocolate
Yuqqatan	Yucatan Peninsula

NOTES ON THE TEXT

In the year 1492 the Genoan sailor Cristoforo Colombo crossed the Atlantic to reach North America, which he believed was India. In that same year Muhammad XII, the last emir of Granada, surrendered to the Spanish Christian forces of the Reconquista, glancing back at the city he had lost from the pass known as the Moor's Last Sigh. With that sigh ended eight hundred years of Islamic rule in Spain, which the Moors called al-Andalus. Spain turned away from the Islamic east and sought a New World in the west.

In the world of *Red Smoking Mirror*, the Reconquest never happened. The Islamic Golden Age of the early Middle Ages, which saw a flowering of learning, culture and religious tolerance, continued into the sixteenth-century Age of Exploration; and Spain, as we know it today, never came into existence. The squabbling emirates of Moorish al-Andalus were unified into one caliphate, ruled from the city of Qurtubah, and the first ships that crossed the Atlantic were crewed by seafaring Moors rather than by Spaniards.

While based on real-life places (and some people), this alternate history is first and foremost a work of fantasy, and is not intended to exactly map onto our world as it is today. In these versions of Spain and Mexico some things developed differently, and even certain physical landmarks have ended up in slightly different places. The volcano that looms above my fictional version of Tenochtitlán, modern-day Mexico City (the Nahuatl name for which is Popocatépetl, or 'smoking mountain'), is around forty miles closer than the one that exists today, and it erupts in 1521, the year the city falls. Old World diseases such as smallpox – which in reality spread through New World populations almost immediately after contact with Europeans – mysteriously take twenty years to reach the Mexica capital, although when they do arrive their impact is just as horrific.

There are other inaccuracies: the Mexica greeting 'good sun' and the farewell 'until the next sun' are my own inventions, as is the Mayan phrase 'our country is green'. The 'caliph's law' was not a historical term from al-Andalus, but refers within these pages, in a rather hazy sense, to the freedoms and legal protections that have grown up over the centuries in fictional Andalus. And the game of backgammon, I discovered after finishing the novel, only dates from the seventeenth century, and did not originate in the Middle East but in Ireland. Perhaps Eli and Moctezuma should be playing draughts or chess; but that's not the game I found them playing. I suppose that in this version of the past, backgammon reached Andalus from Ireland centuries earlier, via North Atlantic trading routes, and was well established there by Eli's time.

Apart from a few minor adjustments, the dates are accurate. Ships from the south-west tip of Europe did cross the sea in 1492 (897 in the Islamic calendar, 13 Knife in the sacred calendar of the Mexica), and Tenochtitlán did fall in 1521 (927, 3 House). It has always astonished me that only twenty-nine years lay between the first Spanish ships landing in the Caribbean and the collapse of Mexica civilisation; a sailor on Colombo's first voyage, or even Colombo himself, could in theory have reached Tenochtitlán with the army of conquistador Hernán Cortés. As far as we know, none did, so I sent Eli Ben Abram to connect these places for me.

The character of Malinala is based on the remarkable figure of La Malinche – born Malintzin and baptised Marina by the Spanish – an Indigenous woman who became the interpreter and mistress of Cortés, without whom the conquest of Tenochtitlán might not have been possible. In Mexico she has variously been denigrated as the great betrayer, celebrated as a feminist icon and regarded as the mother of the first mestizo child, and remains a complex, fascinating and divisive historical figure. In the novel Malinala is born around twenty years later than her real-life counterpart.

Throughout the book I have avoided using the term 'Aztecs', partly because the people of early sixteenth-century Tenochtitlán never called themselves by that name – although the Nahuatl word *aztecatl* was used to refer to 'people from Aztlan', a mythical place of significance in the Mexica origin story – but also because the term felt overly loaded with cultural baggage. I have also avoided 'Culhua-Mexica', which is what they probably did call themselves. The simple term 'Mexica' worked better for the story.

Similarly, my use of 'Moorish' requires explanation. As has been pointed out to me, the term 'Moor' derives from Latin and was used by non-Muslim Europeans to describe Muslims from al-Andalus; the inhabitants of al-Andalus would not have thought of themselves as Moors but simply Muslims. There are many imperfections with the term, which has been used over the centuries to mean Muslim, North African, Black, or combinations of all those identities, but after much consideration I decided to retain it both for its recognisability and for its connotations to a specific time and place: as *Encyclopedia Britannica* puts it, 'The term Moorish continues to be widely used to describe the art, architecture, and high culture of Muslim Andalusia and North Africa dating from the 11th century onward.' In using this term, I recognise that I am writing about that culture from the outside, and through a fictional lens; I only hope that I have done so in a way that conveys the respect, curiosity and admiration I feel for it.

In telling the story I have unavoidably simplified aspects of Mexica society, as the complexity and sophistication of that intriguing civilisation was simply too vast to fit into such a short novel. The 'empire' was not a monolithic block but a Triple Alliance of three *altepetls* or city-states:

Tenochtitlán, Tlacopan and Texcoco. Moctezuma II (whose name really did mean something like 'frowning lord') was not exactly an emperor as we understand the word today – his Nahuatl title, *tlatoani*, meant 'speaker' – and much of the city's day-to-day governance was carried out by a kind of prime minister known as *cihuacoatl*, 'snake woman', who, confusingly, was a man. I regret that they were one character too many for this book. The religion of the Mexica, and its elaborate pantheon of gods, was also far richer and more intricate than this novel can possibly convey, although I hope I have done it some justice with the legend of the Five Suns.

The historical research I carried out, while fascinating, was often brutal and depressing. The chronicles of Cristoforo Colombo, Hernán Cortés and other conquistadors such as Pedro de Alvarado and Francisco Pizarro (who destroyed the Inca Empire) are litanies of massacres, torture, enslavement and cultural desecration, written in a style that is psychopathic in its blandness. To balance out these gold-hungry accounts I read Miguel León-Portilla's *The Broken Spears*, which tells the story of the conquest in the words of contemporary Mexica people, and Camilla Townsend's excellent history *The Fifth Sun*. Other books that aided me were Manuel Aguilar-Moreno's *Handbook to Life in the Aztec World*, Serge Gruzinski's *The Aztecs: Rise and Fall of an Empire*, Matthew Restall's *When Montezuma Met Cortés*, María Rosa Menocal's *The Ornament Of The World*, Richard Fletcher's *Moorish Spain*, Washington Irving's *Tales of the Alhambra*, Alvar Núñez Cabeza de

Vaca's *Chronicle of the Narváez Expedition, The Travels of Ibn Battuta, The Travels of Marco Polo,* and the fairy tales of *One Thousand and One Nights.*

Visually I owe much to the Mexican painter Diego Rivera, whose huge and richly detailed murals in the National Palace of Mexico, depicting pre-Columbian life in the great city of Tenochtitlán and the market at Tlatelolco, are the source of many of the scenes and cityscapes in this book.

In replacing Spaniards with Moors, it was never my intention to suggest that, had the New World been 'discovered' by an Islamic rather than a Christian civilisation, things would have turned out any better for Indigenous Americans. An intolerant strand exists in both religions – as represented by Benmessaoud, whose closest analogue is Cortés – just as coexistence and tolerance exist as a counterbalance. This is something I hope I have portrayed in the culture of al-Andalus, which, at the height of its Golden Age, was enlightened at a time when the Christian nations of Europe were burning heretics at the stake and stamping out heterodoxy. But smallpox and other infectious diseases were carried by Old World populations regardless of their faith, and played a decisive role in devastating Indigenous civilisations. Was there inevitability in the result of an Old World culture – whether Christian, Jewish or Islamic – crashing against a civilisation that, while advanced in many ways, was constitutionally utterly unprepared for what was coming? The history of pandemics alone would suggest that the answer is yes. But this is not supposed to be history; *Red Smoking Mirror* is a fantasy in which I have done my best to portray the uneasy, but nonetheless possible, peace that might have existed between two cultures that were very different but had many things in common.

That peace lasted for almost twenty years, and ended in the year 3 House. Until the next sun.

1444

2023

11 REED

ACKNOWLEDGEMENTS

My thanks to Arts Council England, who funded my initial research and early attempts to write this book. In the course of its development Caroline Williams, Chris Rusbridge, May Abdalla, Amy Rose, Tim Webster, Peter Birchenough, Ron Hutchinson, Alisa Taylor and Caroline Hunt all read iterations of the story, and their combined feedback, helpful criticism and kind support has been invaluable. Special thanks to my agent Jessica Woollard, who wrestled with the unwieldy first draft and helped the story find its form, and *shukran* to Tharik Hussain, who did a close reading of the text and pointed out faults and inaccuracies; those that remain in the book are entirely my responsibility. Thanks to my editor Mark Richards, my copy-editor Sarah Terry, production manager Alex Billington, the book's cartographer Sue Gent, and everyone at Swift Press. Finally, a more abstract thanks to the remembered landscapes and atmospheres of Andalusia, Morocco and Mexico, vivid yet blurred by time, and to the roads I walked that somehow became this novel. *Gracias* to the green Guadalquivir River.

A NOTE ON THE TYPE

This book is set in Espinosa Nova, a typeface created by the designer Cristóbal Henestrosa based on the work of the sixteenth-century Mexican printer and punchcutter Antonio de Espinosa, who is thought to have been the first typographer in North America.